THE
CAT
WHO
SAVED
BOOKS

HarperCollins books may be purchased for educational, business, or sales promotional use. For information, please email the Special Markets Department at SPsales@harpercollins.com.

Originally published as *Hon wo mamorou to suru neko no hanashi* in Japan in 2017 by Shogakukan Inc., English edition arranged with Shogakukan, through Emily Publishing Company, Ltd.

First English Edition published by Pan Macmillan, a division of Macmillan Publishers International Limited, in 2021.

FIRST HARPERVIA EDITION PUBLISHED IN 2021

Designed by Yvonne Chan
Illustration on page iii by Yuko Shimizu

Library of Congress Cataloging-in-Publication Data has been applied for.

ISBN 978-0-06-309572-4
ISBN 978-0-06-322784-2 (Int'l)

22 23 24 25 26 LBC 10 9 8 7 6

THE
CAT
WHO
SAVED
BOOKS

A Novel

SOSUKE
NATSUKAWA

Translated from the Japanese
by Louise Heal Kawai

HarperVia

An Imprint of HarperCollins*Publishers*

CONTENTS

THE
CAT
WHO
SAVED
BOOKS

First things first, Grandpa's gone.

The tale that follows is pretty outrageous, but he knows that one fact is absolutely real.

It's as real as the sun rising in the morning, and his stomach rumbling with hunger at lunchtime. He's tried closing his eyes, blocking his ears, pretending he doesn't know anything, but his grandfather isn't coming back.

Rintaro Natsuki stands there silent and still in the face of this harsh reality. On the outside, Rintaro seems like a calm, collected young man. But some of the people at the funeral find him eerie. He seems too composed for a high school student who has suddenly lost his closest family member. Sticking to the corner of the funeral parlor, Rintaro's eyes stay locked on the portrait of his grandpa.

In truth, Rintaro isn't calm and collected at all. The very idea of death is unfamiliar to him; he can't make the connection between it and his grandfather, a serene man who seemed to exist in a different realm. He never thought death would come for Grandpa, who relished his simple, almost monotonous lifestyle. As Rintaro looks at him lying there, not breathing, he feels detached, as if he were watching a badly performed play.

Now, lying in his white coffin, his grandfather looks just the same as ever—as if nothing has happened at all; as if any moment he might just get up, mumble "Right then," light the paraffin heater, and go make his usual cup of tea. It would have felt perfectly normal to Rintaro, but it doesn't happen. Instead, the old man remains in his casket, his eyes closed and a solemn look on his face.

The chanting of the sutra drones on and mourners pass by in ones and twos, occasionally offering Rintaro their condolences.

First things first, Grandpa's gone.

Reality gradually begins to take root in Rintaro's heart. He finally manages to squeeze out a few words.

"This is messed up, Grandpa."

But there's no reply.

———

Rintaro Natsuki was an ordinary high school student. He was on the short side, pale with rather thick glasses, and rarely spoke.

There was no subject at school he particularly excelled at, and he wasn't good at sports. He was a completely average boy.

Rintaro's parents had split up when he was just a baby. And when his mother passed away right around the time he started primary school, he went to live with his grandfather. It had been just the two of them ever since. Such living arrangements were a little unusual for your typical high school student, but to Rintaro it was just a normal part of his dull everyday existence.

But now that his grandfather had passed away, too, the story became more complicated. His death had been very sudden.

His grandfather was an early riser, but on that bitterly cold winter morning, he wasn't in the kitchen like usual. Thinking it strange, Rintaro poked his head into the dim, tatami-matted room where his grandfather slept. The old man was still tucked inside his futon, having already breathed his last. He didn't look as if he'd been in pain—he seemed to Rintaro more like a sculpture of a person sleeping. In the local doctor's opinion, he'd most probably suffered a heart attack and died quickly.

"He passed away peacefully."

If you combined the kanji character for "go" with the one for "live," you got a strange-looking word meaning "to pass away." Somehow seeing this word was what had shaken Rintaro the most; it struck him as out of place.

The doctor quickly grasped the difficulty of Rintaro's family situation, and in no time an aunt from a distant city turned up.

A kindhearted and efficient woman, she dealt with everything from the paperwork related to the death certificate to organizing the funeral and all the other formalities. As he watched her, Rintaro didn't forget to make sure he looked a bit sad, despite the lingering sense that none of this was real. But no matter how much he thought about it, he just couldn't bring himself to sob in front of his grandfather's funeral photo. It felt absurd to him, and it would be a lie. He could just imagine Grandpa grimacing in his casket, telling Rintaro to stop carrying on.

In the end, Rintaro bid farewell to his grandfather in total silence. All he had left now was a concerned aunt . . . and a bookshop.

Natsuki Books was a tiny secondhand bookshop on the edge of town. The shop didn't lose enough money to be considered a liability, nor did it make enough to be considered a fortune. It wasn't much of an inheritance.

"Hey, Natsuki, you've got some great books here."

The male voice came from behind Rintaro. He didn't turn around.

"Really?" he asked, his eyes fixed on the bookshelves in front of him. The shelves ran from the floor all the way up to the ceiling; they were filled with an impressive number of books.

There was Shakespeare and Wordsworth, Dumas and Stendhal, Faulkner and Hemingway, Golding . . . too many to name. Some of the greatest masterpieces this world has seen—

majestic, dignified tomes stared down at Rintaro. They were all seasoned secondhand books, but none of them too used or worn, no doubt thanks to his grandfather's loving care.

By Rintaro's feet, the similarly seasoned paraffin heater glowed orange, but despite its best efforts, the shop was drafty. Still, Rintaro knew it wasn't only the temperature that was making him feel chilly.

"So how much for these two together?"

Rintaro turned his head and squinted at the books being held out to him.

"Thirty-two hundred yen," he said quietly.

"Your memory's as sharp as ever."

The customer was a boy from the same high school, one year ahead of Rintaro, by the name of Ryota Akiba. He was tall and slim with a cheerful expression, and a calm, self-assured air about him that was quite likable. Along with his strong physique, built up by years of basketball training, he had one of the best brains in his year. In addition, he was the son of the local doctor. This was a boy who had a huge number of extracurricular activities—in other words, he was the exact opposite of Rintaro in every way.

"And these are a bargain."

With that, Akiba began to pile five or six more books next to the register on the desk. Mr. Jack-of-All-Trades was a surprisingly avid reader, and one of Natsuki Books's regular customers.

"You know, this is a really great shop."

"Thank you. Please take your time looking around. It's our closing sale."

It was hard to tell from Rintaro's flat tone if he was serious. Akiba fell silent for a moment.

"It must have been awful for you," he began cautiously, "losing your grandfather."

Akiba swiftly returned his attention to a nearby bookcase and pretended to scour the shelves.

"Seems like just yesterday he was sitting there reading," he continued, casually. "It was so sudden."

"Yes, I feel the same way."

Rintaro sounded as if he was just trying to be polite; even if he did feel the same way, there was no hint of friendliness or sociability in his voice. Akiba didn't seem particularly bothered. He turned to look at the younger boy, who was still staring at the bookshelves.

"But as soon as he passed away, you stopped coming to school. That's not cool. Everyone's worried about you."

"Who's 'everyone'? I can't think of a single person who would be worried about me."

"Oh right, you don't have any friends. Must make life simple. But seriously, your grandpa must be worried sick about you. You've probably got him so anxious, his ghost's still wandering around. How's he supposed to rest in peace? Your grandpa's too old to get this much grief."

His words were harsh, but there was something gentle about the way Akiba spoke them. Because of their shared connection to Natsuki Books, Akiba had a soft spot for the younger boy and his *hikikomori* shut-in tendencies. Even at school, he'd sometimes stop Rintaro for a quick chat. Now his concern was obvious; Akiba had dropped by the bookshop just to check in on him.

Akiba watched Rintaro, who remained tight-lipped. Eventually, Akiba broke the silence.

"So I guess you'll be moving."

"I suppose so," said Rintaro, without taking his eyes off the bookshelves. "I'm going to move in with my aunt."

"Where does she live?"

"I don't know. Before my grandpa died, I'd never met her."

The tone of Rintaro's voice never changed; it was impossible to get a read on him.

With a slight shrug of the shoulders, Akiba dropped his gaze to the books he'd put on the counter.

"Is that why you're having a closing sale?"

"Yes," Rintaro said.

"Pity. This bookshop's collection is one of a kind. These days you rarely come across stuff like a whole set of Proust in hardcover. I finally found those volumes of Romain Rolland's *The Enchanted Soul* I was looking for here."

"Grandpa would be happy to hear that."

"If only he was here to hear it, it would have made his day! You know, being your friend helped me get my hands on so many great books. And now you're going to move."

Akiba's bluntness was his way of expressing concern. Rintaro didn't know the right way to respond, so he just stared over at the wall where there was a huge pile of books. Even for a secondhand bookshop, it was amazing that they could stay in business with the kinds of books they carried, most of which were far from the current trend, and many of which were out of print. Akiba's compliments about the bookshop were not only said to be kind to Rintaro—there was a lot of truth in them.

"When are you moving?" Akiba asked.

"Probably in about a week," Rintaro replied.

"'Probably'? Vague as usual!"

"It doesn't matter. I don't have any choice anyway."

"I guess not."

Akiba shrugged again and looked up at the calendar that hung behind the counter.

"Next week'll be Christmas. That's rough."

"I don't really care about Christmas. Unlike you, I don't have any special plans."

"Thanks for reminding me. Yeah, my schedule sure keeps me busy. It's packed. You know, one of these years I'd really like to try staying up to see Santa Claus on my own watch."

Akiba cracked up laughing, but Rintaro didn't.

"Oh really," he replied quietly.

Akiba pulled a face and sighed.

"I guess if you're moving, there's no point in making an effort to go to school, but don't you think you should leave on a good note? There are people in your class who worry about you, you know."

He glanced at the pile of printouts and the notebooks on the counter. Akiba hadn't brought them; a little earlier, Rintaro's class president had dropped them off.

Her name was Sayo Yuzuki, and she lived nearby. She'd

known Rintaro since primary school. She was a strong, no-nonsense type and not particularly close with the silent, hiki-komori Rintaro. When she'd turned up at the shop and seen Rintaro staring blankly at the shelves, she let out a pointed sigh.

"You look like you don't have a care in the world. Guess the hikikomori life's treating you well, huh? You doing okay?"

Rintaro had shrugged. Sayo frowned, then had turned to Akiba instead.

"Should you really be hanging around here? The basketball club were all looking for you."

She then turned and strode right out of the shop.

She was completely unafraid to be direct with an older boy. That was typical Sayo Yuzuki; it was her way of showing that she cared. Rintaro admired her for it.

"Your class rep is always so driven," Akiba remarked. "She must feel responsible for you. She didn't need to bring you your homework herself . . ."

Though Sayo didn't live far away, Rintaro realized it still must've been a pain to go out of her way when the season was cold enough to see your own breath.

"You can have those for six thousand yen," he said, finally getting to his feet. Akiba raised an eyebrow.

"That's kind of pricey for a closing sale."

"Ten percent off. Can't do more than that. These are literary masterpieces that you're buying."

"Classic Natsuki," Akiba said, laughing. He pulled several notes from his wallet and grabbed his scarf and gloves from the counter. As he secured his bag over his shoulder, he added:

"Come to school tomorrow."

And with his trademark cheerful smile, Akiba left the shop.

Natsuki Books was thrown into silence. Beyond the door the sunset gave off a reddish glow. In the corner, the heater, almost out of paraffin, was beginning to complain.

It was about time to go upstairs and make some dinner. Even when his grandfather had been alive, it had been Rintaro's job, so it wasn't a big deal.

And yet, Rintaro remained motionless, staring at the shop door.

The sun sank lower in the sky, the heater gave out, and cold air began to fill the shop. Still, Rintaro didn't move.

THE FIRST LABYRINTH

The Imprisoner of Books

Natsuki Books was a tiny shop tucked away on a street in the old part of town. It had a rather peculiar layout.

Leading from the front entrance straight through to the back of the store was one single, long aisle. Each side of this aisle was lined with towering stacks of bookshelves reaching all the way to the ceiling, and every shelf was crammed full of books. Retro-style lamps hung overhead, their soft light reflecting off the polished wooden floor.

About halfway down there was a simple wooden desk for handling sales, but besides that and a couple of wooden stools, no other furniture or adornment of any kind. At the back of the store, the aisle ended at a simple wall of bare wood, but when you entered through the front door from bright daylight, you had the impression that the whole place was much deeper than it actually was. Surrounded by walls of books, it felt like entering an endless passageway that disappeared into the darkness beyond.

The image of his grandfather quietly reading a book under a lamp placed on the small desk was seared into Rintaro's memory, its lines drawn simply but with care, like an oil painting by a master artist.

"Books have tremendous power."

That was his grandfather's mantra.

To tell the truth, the old man wasn't much of a talker, but when he got onto the subject of books he would suddenly burst into life. His narrow eyes would crease into a smile, and words flew out of his mouth with passionate energy.

"There are timeless stories, powerful enough to have survived through the ages. Read lots of books like these—they'll be like friends to you. They'll inspire and support you."

Rintaro stared around at the tiny bookshop with its walls of books. Its shelves held none of the current bestsellers. No popular manga or magazines. These days, books didn't even sell the way they used to. Regular customers often expressed concern about the survival of Natsuki Books, but the frail old shopkeeper would just nod a brief "thank you." The complete works of Nietzsche and well-thumbed old collections of T. S. Eliot's poetry remained on display by the front door.

This space that his grandfather had created was the perfect refuge for a boy who tended to be something of a recluse. Rintaro, who had never really fit in at school, got into the habit of coming here and immersing himself in books, voraciously reading anything he could find on the shelves.

In other words, this was Rintaro's safe space, a place where he could find shelter from the outside world. But now, in a few days, Rintaro was going to be forced to leave Natsuki Books forever.

"Grandpa, this is messed up," he whispered.

At that moment, he was brought back to reality by the cheerful ring of the old-fashioned bell that hung on the front door. Normally, it would mean that a customer had come in, but right now the door had its Closed sign up. Outside the sun had set, and beyond the glass door there was nothing but darkness. It felt as if Akiba had only just left, but somehow a great span of time had slipped by.

Deciding the bell had been a trick of his imagination, Rintaro turned his gaze back toward the bookshelves.

"Kinda gloomy in here."

The voice startled him. But when he turned to check the doorway, there was nobody there.

"Pity—you've got quite the collection here, but these books are just fading away in this dingy old place."

Rintaro realized that the voice was coming from deeper inside the store. He spun back around to see . . . nobody. Except, that is, for a tabby cat. It looked like your average ginger tabby—a rather large, plump cat with an orange-and-yellow-striped coat. This particular cat had distinctive stripe markings running from the top of its head down its back and tail—typical of a tabby—but its belly and legs were pure white. Against the dimly lit background, its eyes were two gleaming jade stones. And they were fixed directly on Rintaro.

Rintaro watched as the cat flexed its long, graceful tail.

"You're a cat!"

"Got a problem with that?" asked the cat.

There was no mistaking it—the cat had just spoken.

Although he was shaken, Rintaro managed to scrape together an ounce of calm. He shut his eyes tightly and counted to three. Then he opened them again.

A furry coat, bushy tail, two piercing green eyes, and two neat triangular ears—there was absolutely no doubt about it. It was a cat.

The tabby's whiskers twitched.

"Hey, kid, something wrong with your eyes?" it asked. This wasn't a creature who minced words.

"No, I . . . er . . ." Rintaro scrabbled around for the right thing to say. "My eyesight isn't all that good, but I *can* see that there's a talking cat sitting right in front of me."

"Splendid," the cat said, with a nod. It continued:

"The name's Tiger. Tiger the Tabby."

There was nothing more bizarre than a cat suddenly introducing itself to you, but Rintaro somehow managed to reciprocate.

"I'm Rintaro Natsuki."

"I know. You're the new proprietor of Natsuki Books."

"New proprietor?"

Rintaro was confused. This was the first he'd heard of it.

"I'm sorry to say I'm just a high school boy, a hikikomori," he explained. "My grandpa knew all about books, but he's not around anymore."

"Not a problem," announced the tabby. "My business is with you, the new proprietor."

It fixed Rintaro with slightly narrowed eyes.

"I need your help."

"My help?" Rintaro asked.

"Right. Your help."

"Help with . . . ?"

"There are books that have been imprisoned."

"Books?"

"Are you a parrot? Stop repeating everything I say like some half-wit."

The words landed like a slap across Rintaro's face. The cat, however, paid no attention to his reaction.

"I need to rescue those books." The jade eyes flashed. "And you have to help me."

Rintaro sat for a moment in silence, watching the ginger tabby cat. Then he slowly lifted his right hand and began to fiddle with the frame of his glasses. It was his habit whenever he was thinking.

I must be really tired, he thought.

Rintaro closed his eyes, his hand still on his glasses frame. His grandpa's death and the stress of the funeral, it had all left him exhausted. He must have drifted off to sleep without realizing it and now he was dreaming. Convinced by his own logic, he opened his eyes again. But there was still a tabby cat sitting calmly right in front of him.

Okay, now I have a problem.

Come to think of it, I've been sitting staring at these bookshelves for days now.

I've really fallen behind on my reading . . .

Now where did I leave that copy of Candide *I just started?*

All sorts of random thoughts began to pop into his head.

"Are you listening, Mr. Proprietor?"

The tabby cat's sharp tone pierced the bubble of Rintaro's thoughts.

"Look, kid, I'll say it one more time. I need you to help me save those books."

"You say you need me, but . . ."

Rintaro was struggling to find the right words.

"I'm useless. Like I said, I'm just a high school hikikomori," he said earnestly, from his seat behind the register.

For some reason, he couldn't make himself lie to this talking tabby cat.

"No problem. I already knew you were a miserable, good-for-nothing shut-in," the cat sneered. "But I still have a favor to ask you."

"If you already knew that, then why are you asking for my help? There must be millions of people who could do a better job than me," Rintaro said.

"Goes without saying."

"And I've just lost my grandpa. I'm feeling pretty depressed right now."

"I get that."

"So then why—"

"Don't you like books?"

The tabby cat's deep voice brushed off all Rintaro's protests. It was gentler now, but also filled with determination. Rintaro didn't really understand what the cat was talking about, but its strong presence and the power of its speech seemed to rob him of all reason.

The jade eyes stared straight into Rintaro's.

"Yes . . . Yes, of course I like books."

"Then what's stopping you?"

Everything about the tabby cat was bold and confident—so different from Rintaro himself. The boy began to fiddle with his glasses frame again, desperately trying to figure out what was going on. But there was no explanation that made any sense.

"The important stuff is always difficult to understand, Mr. Proprietor," said the cat, as if reading Rintaro's thoughts. "Most people don't get that obvious truth. They just go about their everyday lives, and yet 'it is only with the heart that one can see rightly; what is essential is invisible to the eye.'"

"Well!" Rintaro's eyes widened. "I never expected to hear a cat quoting *The Little Prince*."

"Not into Saint-Exupéry?"

"He's one of my favorite authors," Rintaro replied, pointing to a nearby shelf, "but I think I like *Night Flight* best. And I couldn't put *Southern Mail* down."

"Splendid," said the tabby with a grin.

The cat's composure brought a strong wave of nostalgia over the boy. Somehow it reminded him of his grandfather, except Grandpa had never been this talkative.

"So you'll help me?"

Rintaro shrugged.

"Am I allowed to refuse?"

"You are," replied the cat right away, and then added crankily, "but I will be bitterly disappointed if you do."

Rintaro grimaced slightly.

So this cat turns up out of nowhere, asking for help, then says it's going to be bitterly disappointed if I don't agree . . .

It just wasn't reasonable, yet there was something appealing about the cat's plainspoken style—he couldn't get too mad at it. On reflection, this cat probably was a lot like his grandpa after all.

"So what do you need me to do?"

"Follow me."

"Where to?"

"Come on!"

The cat turned around and headed not in the direction of the front door, but toward the shadows at the far end of the store. Rather confused, Rintaro followed, but he'd barely taken more than a few steps before a very curious feeling of vertigo came over him. Natsuki Books was long and narrow; he had expected to run into the wall at the back in another few steps. But today, there was no dead end. The aisle lined with its towering walls of bookcases just kept going. The old-fashioned lamps overhead also seemed to repeat infinitely. As they walked, Rintaro noticed that the shelves were filled with books he'd never seen before. Many of them were different from the usual bound books of today. They'd left behind old secondhand paperbacks and moved on to beautiful leather-bound tomes, embossed with gold; the passageway had become a gallery of gorgeous books.

"Th . . . This . . . I, er . . ."

Rintaro began to ramble incoherently. The cat looked over its shoulder at him.

"Are you frightened, Mr. Proprietor? If you're going to bail on me, then now's your chance."

"I was just wondering when the store got all these new books," Rintaro replied, peering into the distance, then looking down at the cat. "With all these new titles to read, I don't think I'm ready to leave the hikikomori life just yet. Maybe I'll ask my aunt if we can delay the move."

"Hmm. Your sense of humor leaves something to be desired, but your heart is in the right place. This world throws all kinds of obstacles at us; we are forced to endure so much that is absurd. Our best weapon for fighting all the pain and trouble in the world isn't logic or violence. It's humor."

Having dispensed this nugget of wisdom in the style of some ancient philosopher, the tabby cat padded off again down the corridor.

"Let's go, Mr. Proprietor."

Rintaro followed obediently.

Soon the bookshelves on each side were stocked with an assortment of thick volumes that were totally unfamiliar to him. As the boy and the cat made their way forward, the passageway became infused with a faint, bluish glow. It gradually brightened, until eventually the whole space was filled with a blinding white light.

―――――――

He saw bright sunlight and trees swaying gently.

The white light faded, and Rintaro found himself surrounded by pleasant scenery. At his feet, flagstones gleamed brightly in the sunshine. Overhead, the branches of a large mimosa silk tree swayed in the breeze, creating glittery showers of sunbeams. And beyond those . . . Rintaro screwed up his eyes to try to make it out.

"A gate?"

A short distance away, at the top of a flight of stone steps, was a magnificent *yakuimon* roofed gateway. Its roof was made with traditional decorative tiles, and its great wooden doors polished to a fine gloss, but the overall feeling was of something vaguely oppressive. Rintaro looked left and right. In both directions, a perfectly even wall continued as far as the eye could see. Next to the main gate was a smaller door in the wall; the nameplate appeared to be blank.

20

The regular flagstones, stretching away into the distance, were spotless. Not so much as a fallen leaf marred their surface. The particles of light that filtered through the spaces between the roof and the trees sparkled like dancing water droplets.

There was not a soul in sight.

"We're here," said the cat. "This is our destination."

"This is where the books are?"

"They're imprisoned behind there."

Rintaro took another look at the magnificent gate and the mimosa tree above. Its giant branches were covered in cottony blossoms. That was strange. It was December, which made this a very unusual mimosa indeed. But then again, from the outset everything he had seen today had defied common sense. At this point it seemed hardly worth taking issue with these hardy flowers.

"What an impressive mansion. This gate alone is about the size of our bookshop," Rintaro said.

"Don't worry. It's all a bluff. Behind a big impressive gate lives many a sorry excuse for a man."

"Well, from the point of view of a high school student who lives in a sorry excuse for a house, I wouldn't say no to a gate like this."

"Make the most of your freedom to stand around kvetching," said the cat. "If we don't manage to rescue those books, you'll be stuck in this labyrinth forever."

Rintaro was flabbergasted.

". . . I, er . . . you seem to have left that part out."

"Well, obviously, if I'd told you that bit before, you'd never have agreed to come. Sometimes ignorance is bliss."

"That's a dirty trick."

"Is it though? Sitting there with your miserable face, it was pretty clear you had nothing much to lose."

The cat's words were pure venom. *So this is what they mean by "brutally honest,"* Rintaro thought. He stared up at the gloriously blue sky as he formulated his response.

"I don't get a kick out of hurting dumb animals, but . . ."

He paused to adjust his glasses.

". . . right now, I've got this overwhelming desire to grab you by the scruff of your neck and shake you."

"Splendid. That's the spirit!"

With utter composure, the cat began to climb the steps to the gate. Rintaro scrambled after it.

"Just wondering—what happens if we can't get back?"

"We'll probably be doomed to walk the length of this wall for eternity. Then again, I've never gotten stuck here before, so I don't really know," the cat admitted.

"That's not good."

Rintaro stopped on the top step, right before the massive wooden doors.

"So what exactly do I need to do?"

"Just talk to the lord of the manor."

"And then?"

"If you manage to persuade him, then we're done."

"That's it?"

Rintaro looked surprised. But the cat wasn't finished.

"I've got one more assignment for you," it announced in a pompous tone. "Would you mind pressing the doorbell?"

Rintaro did as requested.

⸻

Out from the small door by the gate came an attractive woman dressed in a simple indigo kimono. From her restrained demeanor, you would have guessed she was an old lady, but her exact age was hard to judge. There was no air of warmth about her, and she had dead eyes. From the red ornamental hairpin stuck in her chignon and the porcelain whiteness of her skin, she could easily have been mistaken for an exquisite Japanese doll.

Rintaro couldn't bring himself to speak.

"May I help you?" she said in a monotone voice.

The cat took over from the flustered boy.

"We would like to meet with your husband."

The woman turned her lifeless eyes onto the cat. Rintaro felt a nervous chill run through him, but both the cat and the woman seemed completely unfazed.

"My husband is a busy man. Unexpected visitors—"

The cat cut her off.

"This is a matter of great importance. And time sensitive, too. Please let him know we're here."

"Every day my husband receives visits from people who claim they have urgent and important business with him, but

23

he's far too busy with his TV and radio appearances. It's not the kind of schedule that permits him to meet with unannounced guests. Please come back another time."

"We don't have time for that."

The determination in the tabby's voice stopped the woman in her tracks. The cat seized the moment.

"We're here to discuss book matters—this young man here has vital information for your husband. I'm sure he'll be able to find time for us."

The cat's manner appeared to have an effect on the kimono-clad woman. She stood for a while, apparently considering its words. Then finally, with a cursory "Wait here," she gave a quick bow and disappeared back through the door.

Rintaro stared at the cat.

"Who has 'vital information'?" he demanded.

"Let's not worry about the details for now. As I see it, we're using the bluffer's own tactics to stand up to him. Bluffing the bluffer, if you like. We'll work out what we're going to say once we get inside."

"That's so . . . !"

Rintaro hesitated a moment.

". . . *reassuring*," he spat.

The woman soon reappeared. She bowed to the boy and the cat, before addressing them in the same monotone.

"This way, please."

———

On the other side of the gate stood a magnificent mansion, the likes of which Rintaro had never seen.

They walked across the neat flagstones, passed through the latticed front door, and took off their shoes at the *genkan* entrance foyer. Then they stepped up into a corridor with a polished wood floor. This led into the *engawa* veranda that surrounded the house, which in turn led into a kind of connecting bridge that took them over toward an annex building.

From the connecting bridge they could see extensive Japanese-style gardens. Birds chirped in the trees, and the neatly pruned azalea bushes were in full flower—once again, blooming out of season.

"Didn't you say the house would be modest?" said Rintaro.

"I was speaking allegorically. Stop prattling on. Save your breath."

Rintaro and the cat were whispering furiously to each other, but the woman leading the way didn't say a single word.

As they walked, the scenery began to change. What had at first appeared to be a traditional Japanese residence underwent a very bizarre transformation.

First, the wooden veranda became a marble staircase, and the extensive gardens that at one moment they had been viewing from the balustrade of a Chinese arched bridge suddenly became those of a Western palace, dotted with exquisite stone fountains and nude statues. And just ahead, beyond Japanese *fusuma* paper doors painted with delicate bamboo designs, they could see glittering chandeliers and brightly painted vases sitting on art deco tea tables.

"I don't know about you but I'm getting a headache," said Rintaro.

"Same here."

It was the first time the cat had ever agreed with him.

"It's like they threw a whole bunch of stuff from all over the world together in one place," Rintaro continued.

"It looks like it's full, but in fact it's empty."

The cat's response was very Zen.

"There's no philosophy behind it and no taste. No matter how rich and wonderful it all looks on the outside, when you take off the lid and look inside there's nothing but a jumble of borrowed junk. It's the worst kind of ignorance."

"I think that's going too far," said Rintaro.

"I'm just telling it like it is. And anyway, it's really common. You see it everywhere, every day."

"This mansion," said the woman, gently interrupting the cat, "has been decorated to reflect my husband's rich and varied wealth of experiences and excellent judgment. I imagine it may be beyond your understanding."

For a split second, Rintaro thought this was some kind of joke. The woman was walking ahead so he couldn't see her face, but then he realized she sounded far from amused.

There was a strange tension in the air as they advanced farther and farther into the residence. Corridors, staircases, connecting verandas—the distance they were covering was extraordinary. And all the while they passed ivory carvings mixed in among Japanese ink paintings, statues of Venus, katana

26

swords. There seemed to be no rhyme or reason behind the arrangement of any of these ornaments.

The direction they were moving seemed to change without warning, so that they had absolutely no idea where they were in the midst of the chaos.

From time to time, the woman would turn and call over her shoulder, "Are you all right?" Rintaro and his tabby friend had no choice but to nod and follow.

"Even if we were told to leave now, I'm not sure that I would be able to find my way back," whispered Rintaro.

"Don't worry, Mr. Proprietor," said the cat, glancing up at the boy. "I have no idea how to get out of here either."

As usual, the cat didn't sugarcoat the truth.

At last, they came to the end of their long journey. They walked down one final, red-carpeted corridor, at the far end of which was a checkered fusuma sliding door. The woman stopped in front of it.

"Thank you for your patience," she said, placing her hand lightly on the door. It slid open. Rintaro's eyes grew wide as he took in the contents of the room beyond.

It was a massive hall, its walls, floor, and ceiling all painted white. The whiteness made it impossible to gauge the exact size of the space, but at the very least Rintaro could tell that it was unlike anything he had seen before. The ceiling was as high as a school gymnasium's, and the walls seemed to go on forever.

The hall was filled with neat rows of white-painted display

cases. Each of these glass-fronted cases was taller than Rintaro and arranged in what must have been around twenty rows, all perfectly aligned. But even though the start of each row was visible, they stretched farther back than the eye could see.

However, what amazed Rintaro more than anything wasn't the size or the number of these display cases; it was their contents. Every single case was filled with books. Every shelf of every case was stuffed full. He couldn't tell exactly how many of these giant bookcases there were, or the total number of books being stored here, but one thing he knew: the figure must be mind-boggling.

"Wow!"

He began to walk down one of the rows of cases. It was breathtaking. There was a huge variety of books from all different periods. Literature, philosophy, poetry, collections of letters, diaries—every genre you could imagine. The quality and the number were overwhelming.

And yet every single book appeared to be brand new. There was not a mark to be seen on any of them—they were beautiful.

"I've never seen such an amazing collection," said Rintaro.

"I'm delighted to hear that."

The voice resounded from somewhere deep among the display cases.

Rintaro followed the source of the voice through the room from bookcase to bookcase, and finally came across a tall man sitting in a white chair.

He wore a suit in the exact same bright white as the polished floor. Sitting with crossed legs in a small swivel chair, his eyes were fixed on the thick book open on his lap. The cases on the far side of his chair had no books in them yet. In other words, they had come to the farthest point of the collection, deep inside the storeroom.

"Welcome to my study."

The man glanced up at Rintaro.

He had a gentle smile, but a keen gaze, revealing a man of great sophistication.

Rintaro recalled that the woman had mentioned appearances on television and radio. This man looked like someone you would see on TV.

"He looks really smart," muttered Rintaro to the cat.

"Are you that easily intimidated? Stay strong!"

The man's gaze switched from Rintaro to the cat.

"Are you the ones here to discuss 'book matters'?"

"Well, um . . ."

The man's eyes flashed coldly at Rintaro's tepid response.

"If you'll excuse me, I'm rather busy. I really don't have the time to sit around idly chatting with some boy—particularly one who turns up unannounced, doesn't even bother to introduce himself, and then just stands there like a deer in the headlights."

"Oh, sorry. My name's Rintaro Natsuki." Hurriedly readjusting his posture, Rintaro gave a deep bow. "Please excuse us for intruding."

"I see," replied the man with narrowed eyes. "Now what is this vital information you have for me? If it has to do with books, then I suppose I'd like to hear it."

Rintaro had been put on the spot, and he had nothing to say. The vital information had never existed. He looked desperately at the cat.

"We've come to free your books." The cat's white whiskers twitched as it spoke.

The man's eyes narrowed farther as he looked down at the cat. There was something menacing in his gaze.

"I really don't have a minute to spare. I have my TV and radio appearances to prepare for, and so many lectures and articles to write. I do manage to squeeze out some time to cast my eyes over these books—my collection comes from all over the world. But I don't have time to deal with raving lunatics."

He sighed deeply, making a show of looking at his wristwatch.

"I've already wasted two precious minutes listening to you. If you've finished, I'd like you to leave now."

But the cat wasn't going to give up that easily.

"We're not done talking."

"I already told you to leave." The man glared at the tenacious tabby. "I've only read sixty-five of my hundred-book quota so far. Get out."

"A hundred books?" Rintaro couldn't help but ask. "You read a hundred books a year?"

"Not a year," the man replied, theatrically turning the next page in his book.

"A month," he continued, with great pomposity. "And that is why I'm so busy. I welcomed you, thinking you were bringing me news that might be to my benefit, but clearly, I was mistaken. If you continue to waste my time, I will have you thrown out. Of course, once you leave this room, I have no idea whether the two of you will ever be able to find your way out again, but that's no concern of mine."

His tone was icy. In the abrupt silence that followed, the only sound was the rustle of pages turning. The tabby cat glared at him aggressively, but the man was completely unperturbed. It was as if he'd completely forgotten his visitors' existence.

There was nothing more to be said. Rintaro was looking around helplessly when his gaze fell on one of the display cases. The man's collection really was varied, or perhaps, simply random; the shelves were filled not only with regular books, but also magazines, maps, dictionaries. Nothing was arranged in any sequence, or relating to any particular field.

Natsuki Books also had a remarkable collection, but Rintaro's grandpa had always had some kind of system to his shelf arrangement. In contrast, despite its impressive appearance, the man's collection was, in fact, total chaos.

Rintaro took a deep breath.

"Have you read all of Nietzsche?"

He was looking at the bookcase right behind the man. All of Nietzsche's works, including the famous *Thus Spoke Zarathustra*, along with collections of his letters, were lined up inside the glass case.

"I like Nietzsche, too," he added.

"There are people all over the world who claim to like Nietzsche," replied the man, without lifting his head from his book. "However, there are very few people who say this after having read all his work. They've seen the odd quotation or some watered-down, abridged version. They try Nietzsche on for size like some fashionable overcoat. Are you one of those, too?"

Rintaro was quick to respond.

"'Scholars who at bottom do little nowadays but thumb books . . . ultimately lose entirely their capacity to think for themselves. When they don't thumb, they don't think.'"

The man slowly lifted his head from his book.

"Nietzsche really was a straight talker," continued Rintaro, hastily. "That's why I like him."

Without moving a muscle, the man sat and observed his rather timid conversation partner. His eyes were filled with contempt, but somewhere deep inside was a faint glimmer of interest. Finally, he closed his book.

"All right. I may be able to spare you a little of my time."

The glacial atmosphere thawed a little. The cat looked at Rintaro with a good measure of surprise, but Rintaro had no time right now for his feline friend. Under the pressure of the man's expression, he had to fight the instinct to run. He raised his voice.

"We came here because we heard you have lots of books imprisoned."

"You shouldn't believe everything you hear. See for yourself. I just have one copy of each book that I've read. I'm taking great care of them."

"Each book that you've read? Are all the books here ones you've already read?"

"Naturally." He gestured around the cavernous hall. "From the first bookcase by the door where you came in, all the way to where I'm sitting now—fifty-seven thousand six hundred and twenty-two books. That's the number I have read thus far."

"Fifty-seven thousand—"

The man gave a half smile.

"It's not that shocking. All the intellectual leaders of our time, such as myself, are constantly reading. It's vital for us always to be brushing up on our philosophy and expanding our knowledge. Books have made me the man I am today. They're my dear companions. And thus, I'm completely bewildered by you two, coming here with your false accusations."

He nonchalantly uncrossed his long legs and shot the boy a look. Rintaro was hit by a seething wave of self-importance and pride so strong he thought it would knock him off his feet. Nevertheless, he stood his ground—Rintaro was genuinely perplexed.

"But then why are you keeping your books like that?"

The glass cases were all tightly shut, their handles padlocked together. Rintaro still didn't understand the exact meaning of the cat's words—"books that have been imprisoned"—but he did know that this was no way to display books. The cases were beautiful but suffocating.

"It's unnatural," Rintaro said.

The man frowned.

"These books are important to me. I love books. What's unnatural about guarding your treasure?"

"Because you're treating them like museum pieces. Putting

a great big padlock on them like that—they're your books but you can't even get to them."

"Get to them? Why would I want to do that? I've already read them."

Now Rintaro was even more confused than the man.

"You're done after reading them once? You don't want to reread—"

"Reread them? Are you an idiot?"

The words reverberated through the great hall. The man in the white suit reached out a long, slender finger and gently touched the glass of the nearest display case.

"Haven't you been listening to anything I've said? I'm too busy reading new books. It's already difficult enough to reach my monthly quota. I don't have spare time to reread things."

"So you never reread your books?" said Rintaro, taken aback.

"Of course not." The man seemed genuinely shocked. He shook his head.

"I'm going to have to chalk your stupidity up to your age. Otherwise, the inanity of these last three minutes is going to throw me into despair. The world is *full* of books, you agree? It's impossible to count the number of books that have been, and are still being, written. To find the time to read the same books over again—well, it's just inconceivable."

The words echoed hollowly in the cavernous space. Rintaro began to feel light-headed and queasy.

"The world is full of 'readers,'" the man went on. "But a

person of *my* standing is required to read far more books than the average reader. Someone who has read twenty thousand books is much more valuable than someone who has read only ten thousand. And so why would I reread the same book when there are still piles of books that need to be read? Out of the question! Ridiculous waste of time!"

Something gleamed in the man's narrowed eyes. It was a gleam that came from such utter self-confidence that it had begun to border on insanity.

At a loss for words, Rintaro held his tongue and watched.

What the man was saying was not completely unreasonable. The building blocks of his argument, however distorted or misshapen they may be, had been neatly arranged into a great, unbroken wall. He'd built his case, and because the man was so proud, so sure of himself, it was solid and unshakable.

"Books have tremendous power."

That was his grandpa's pet phrase. And now the man in front of Rintaro was claiming that books had made him the man he was today—it sounded to Rintaro as if the two men were saying the same thing.

And yet . . .

Rintaro reached up and began to fiddle with the frame of his glasses. There was something very different about this man; his words were twisted somehow. If he had been Rintaro's grandpa, he would have taken the time to respond to the boy's questions calmly and kindly.

"I'm extremely busy," the man repeated.

And with that, he turned his chair to face away from his visitors and toward the bookshelves. He opened his book again, then raised one hand to point in the direction of the door.

"Please leave."

Rintaro didn't move. The cat, too, appeared to be deep in thought. The silence became oppressive. The man went back to turning the pages of his book. The dry, rustling sound filled the cavernous hall.

Suddenly there was a different, swishing sound. The white fusuma door had slid open, but there was no one on the other side, no sign of the woman who had brought them here. All they could see was a deep, sinister darkness. Rintaro shuddered.

"Think about it, Mr. Proprietor," whispered the cat. "This one is only a tough rival because there's truth in what he says."

"Truth?"

"Right. This labyrinth runs on the power of truth. And it doesn't matter how contorted that truth may be—as long as personal conviction is involved, it won't collapse easily. But not *everything* he says is true."

The cat took a measured pace forward.

"He has a weak spot," it hissed. "He's very skilled at spouting heaps of words, but they can't all be true. There's got to be a lie in there somewhere."

"A lie?"

Something in the atmosphere changed. Rintaro turned to look at the door. Beyond the darkness a wind had begun to blow. Or rather, there was a wind blowing through the hall, toward the darkness, easing Rintaro and the cat toward the fusuma door. This wind was steadily increasing in strength, its destination that mysterious black vortex of emptiness outside. A chill ran down Rintaro's spine.

He turned back to see that the man was still engrossed in his book as if nothing were happening. It looked as if he'd nearly reached the end of that great thick volume . . . And after he turned the last page, that finished book would be no more than a decorative object somewhere in the chaos of this book vault. Stuffed into one of these showy glass-fronted cases. Locked up, never to be handled again.

All these books really were imprisoned.

The wind had begun to howl now, and Rintaro couldn't hear the cat, who was trying to tell him something.

But Rintaro's attention was still focused on the books. He turned to the man.

"Something's not right." He'd only mustered a faint mutter, but the man's shoulders twitched in response.

"I'm sure you're lying."

This time Rintaro's voice was louder, and the man turned to glower at him. But Rintaro refused to buckle under the force of his glare.

"You're lying to us. You say that you love books, but that's not true."

"What a thing to say." The man's reply was too quick. "You're just a kid. Before you incur the wrath of your superior, you'd better take that offensive eyesore of a cat and get the hell out of here."

"You don't love books at all," repeated Rintaro, standing up straighter and looking the man directly in the eyes. His opponent noticeably flinched.

"On what evidence—"

"Just look around you."

Rintaro's voice came out more powerfully than he'd expected. But it wasn't only the force of his voice; it was that he knew exactly what to say.

"I agree that there's an amazing number of books here. I'm sure it's rare to find such a variety in one place. And you even have precious old books that are really difficult to find these days. But that's all."

"All?"

"Take for example this ten-volume edition here: *The D'Artagnan Romances*."

Rintaro pointed to a row of ten beautifully bound books on a shelf to his left. The titles stood out boldly in gold lettering against a white background. Alexandre Dumas's greatest works, translated into Japanese, were enshrined in a display case.

"It's not every day you get the chance to see all these works together like this. All ten books looking as if they've never been opened, in perfect condition. Look at the size of these volumes. No matter how carefully you read them, they must surely end up with a mark or two, perhaps even a bent spine. And yet they look as if they have only just been delivered, brand new."

"Books are treasures to me. I read each book with the

utmost care and place it into the display case when I finish. It's a part of my daily routine, and it gives me great pleasure."

"Then where's volume eleven?"

The man's eyebrow twitched.

"In the Japanese translation, *The D'Artagnan Romances* is an eleven-volume set. The final volume, *Farewell to the Sword*, is missing," Rintaro said, causing the man to freeze.

Rintaro ignored him. He gestured at the shelf to his right.

"Over there you have *Jean-Christophe* by Rolland. I can see the first and the last groupings of volumes, but there should be a middle grouping, too. And what about *The Chronicles of Narnia*? Where's *The Horse and His Boy*? You say that books are your treasures, but it doesn't look that way. On the surface, everything seems to be in perfect order, but when you look closely, these shelves are a mess."

Rintaro looked up at the ceiling of the great hall. At some point during his speech, the raging wind had dropped to a breeze.

"This isn't a library for holding your precious books. They're for showing off whatever books you managed to get your hands on. The whole place is nothing but a showroom."

He paused a moment, then turned to look the man straight in the eye.

"People who truly love books don't treat them this way."

Into his mind had slipped a memory of his grandpa, smiling contentedly as he read one of his favorites over and over until it fell apart. He'd been completely absorbed in every story.

Rintaro's grandpa had always handled the books in his store with the greatest of care, but that didn't mean he treated them as decorations. He hadn't been obsessed with having some sort of gorgeous exhibition—he had concentrated on creating a well-maintained space filled with the kind of books people wanted to reach out and pick up, no matter how old or well-worn they might be. That was what had made Rintaro a reader.

Rintaro repeated something his grandpa had told him that had always stuck with him.

"It's good to read lots of books, but make no mistake . . ."

The man in the white suit flinched again, but he didn't speak. In the silence, Rintaro found his memories turning ever more fluidly into words.

". . . Books have tremendous power. But take care. It's the book that holds the power, not you."

That's what his grandpa had said back when Rintaro was skipping school and spending his days frenziedly raiding the shelves of Natsuki Books. Rintaro would shut himself away between the walls of books, immersed in the world of letters and gradually losing all interest in the outside world. The normally taciturn old man would warn his grandson:

"It's not true that the more you read, the more you see of the world. No matter how much knowledge you cram into your head, unless you think with your own mind, walk with your own feet, the knowledge you acquire will never be anything more than empty and borrowed."

Rintaro would respond with a shrug, but his grandpa calmly continued:

"Books can't live your life for you. The reader who forgets to walk on his own two feet is like an old encyclopedia, his head stuffed with out-of-date information. Unless someone else opens it up, it's nothing but a useless antique."

The old man gently ruffled the boy's hair.

"Do you want to end up a walking encyclopedia?" he teased.

Rintaro couldn't recall how he'd answered. But he did remember it wasn't long after that that he started going to school again.

Even so, he still tended to burrow himself completely in the world of books. His grandpa would sit there, sipping at his cup of tea, and issue him the occasional reminder:

"It's all very well to read a book, but when you've finished, it's time to set foot in the world."

It finally occurred to Rintaro that this was his grandpa's awkward way of encouraging him, of guiding him—he had done his best.

The man in white broke into Rintaro's thoughts.

"But that's how I've elevated my status—by collecting all these books. The more books you have, the more powerful you are. That's how I got to where I am."

"And is that why you've imprisoned them? To show them off as if their power belongs entirely to you?" Rintaro said.

"What are you talking about?"

"You think you're so impressive—you built this ridiculous, pretentious showroom just so that everyone can see how many books you've read."

"Shut up!"

The man couldn't sit still any longer. Abandoning all pretense of reading his book, he glared angrily at Rintaro.

"What would a brat like you know?"

Beads of sweat had appeared on his forehead.

"Who does society value more—the man who reads the same book ten times, or the one who reads ten books once each?" he went on. "Obviously, the more books you read, the more respect you get. The more well-read you are, the more fascinating and attractive people find you. Am I wrong?"

"I couldn't tell you if you're right or wrong. But that's not what I'm talking about."

"What?" The man was totally confused.

"What society demands, what kind of people get respect— I'm not talking about any of that."

"So what are you—"

"All I'm saying is that you don't love books. The only thing you love is yourself. As I think I already mentioned, people who truly love books don't treat them this way."

Once again, a deep silence fell over the room. The man seemed to have turned to stone. He didn't move from his spot in the chair; his hands still grasped his open book. Previously so stuck up and arrogant, it looked as if he had shrunk a whole size smaller.

The slight breeze dropped away, and the room became still. Rintaro turned to see that the fusuma door had closed again.

"Do y—"

The man opened his mouth to speak, but stopped again right away. The room was quiet again as he searched for the right words. Finally, he seemed to settle on a phrase.

"Do you love books?"

It wasn't the abruptness of the question that surprised Rintaro. It was the sincere light that radiated from the man's eyes. It was such a difference from the coldness, the overbearing attitude he had demonstrated until now. It was a light that showed a new kind of consideration, along with a deep sense of loneliness.

"Despite everything, do you still love books?"

The phrase "despite everything" held so much meaning. Rintaro took a moment to consider all its implications.

"I do," he said firmly.

"Me, too."

The man's voice was softer; the steely edge was gone. He sounded almost spiritual.

Suddenly Rintaro heard a curious sound that reminded him of the gentle whispering of a breeze. He looked around to see that the whole room had begun to transform. All the giant display cases—once the man in white's pride and joy—were beginning to collapse like sandcastles. One by one, the books soared into the air, like birds taking flight.

"I really do love books, you know."

And with that, the man carefully closed the book he'd been reading, tucked it under his arm, and stood up. As he did so, the nearest display case crumbled into dust, its books now a flock of migrating birds. Rintaro watched in awe as the whole room filled with flapping books. The man in white looked at him.

"You're an impressive young man."

"I'm not really—"

The man held up a hand to cut him off, then glanced to the side.

"It turns out you invited in the most troublesome guests," he said, with a smile.

Rintaro realized he was addressing the woman in the kimono, who had materialized out of nowhere. She looked different. Back when she'd met them at the gate, she'd had no expression, almost as if she were wearing a mask. Now there was a smile on her face.

"You don't need any help getting home. You'll find your way," said the man.

His voice rang out over the flapping of the winged books.

As the last of the bookcases turned to dust, a pale, bluish light began to fill the room, reflecting off the pages of the migrating books and turning the air into a whirl of whiteness.

The man looked at his wristwatch.

"Well, you certainly took up a lot of my time. But I must confess it was the most enjoyable I've ever spent. I'm very grateful to you."

The woman handed him a white hat, which he placed on his head, and he turned to leave.

"Au revoir," he said.

The woman beside him had just started to lower her head in a bow when a sudden flash turned everything blinding white.

At 7:00 a.m. the following day, Rintaro was in the kitchen. He finished his breakfast and opened the door to the bookshop. He went in, turning on the lights, raising the window blinds, and letting some air into the space. The cold breeze that poured in blew away the old, stagnant air. Rintaro swept off the stone steps that led to the door, then switched his broom for a feather duster and set to work dusting off the bookshelves.

This routine was one his grandfather had performed every morning. It was the same scene he'd observed every morning before going to school, but today was the first time he'd ever performed the routine himself. He'd picked up and read so many of the books in there, but he'd never once helped with the cleaning.

What on earth are you doing? said a voice inside his head.

But then a different voice laughed.

It's fine, it replied.

Both voices were Rintaro's own, and it was true that he had no idea what he was doing. He let out a sigh, and his breath was white in the bright but chilly morning air.

He stared gloomily at the bookshelves, wondering why he'd started dusting them at all. Further back in his mind lingered the memory of yesterday's strange adventure.

"That was excellent work, Mr. Proprietor."

The rich voice came from a tabby cat with a fine coat of fur.

Rintaro pulled a face as he watched the cat stroll toward him through the bookshop's narrow space, its jade green eyes creased into a smile.

"What's up?" it asked him.

"I'm not used to being praised for anything," Rintaro replied.

"It's good to be humble. But there's such a thing as taking it too far."

The cat continued toward him.

"Your words managed to move somebody. That's a fact. And you succeeded in releasing a huge number of imprisoned books, at the same time making it back home yourself. Without your words, we would never have been able to return and would have ended up wandering that freaky house for eternity."

The thought was terrifying, but the cat spoke in its usual nonchalant way. Rintaro spotted the hint of a smile in its eyes.

"Excellent work. We've managed to make it through the first labyrinth."

"You're welcome . . . Huh?" Rintaro broke off and stared at the cat. "What do you mean, '*first* labyrinth'?"

"Oh, it's nothing. Don't worry about it."

Rintaro was standing in the center of Natsuki Books. The tabby cat slipped between his legs and headed toward the back wall once again.

"Wait a minute! You say don't worry about it, but— Hey, you!"

"I told you my name is Tiger the Tabby. Try to remember."

46

The cat smiled over its shoulder.

"It really was outstanding work."

"Don't change the subject."

Rintaro had no sooner uttered these words than the extra passageway at the back of the bookshop dissolved into a white light and he found himself standing alone before the wooden wall. It was a whole day since the adventure, but somehow, he still felt as if he were dreaming.

Outstanding work, huh?

He could still hear the tabby's voice in his ears.

No one had ever praised him so directly before. People had always laughed at Rintaro, called him spineless or weak. He was used to being avoided because he was always so glum, but now he was strangely unsettled by these new descriptions being thrown at him. He was so unsettled that he found himself unable to sit down with a book in the dim shop as usual. He grabbed the duster again instead and put all his energy into cleaning off those shelves.

He'd just about finished when he heard the front doorbell. He looked over to see Sayo Yuzuki, his neighbor and class rep, wrapped in a warm, red scarf. She peered into the bookshop and raised one perfectly shaped eyebrow when she saw Rintaro standing there.

"What are you doing?"

"What do you . . . ?"

For a moment he was confused, but then when he thought about it, he realized he should have been the one asking her the question.

"It's seven in the morning. What are you doing here, Sayo?"

"I'm going to band practice. I always leave around now."

She raised her left hand to show him a black instrument case.

"And as I was passing, I happened to notice that Natsuki Books, which ought to have been closed, was actually open. I popped in to see what was going on."

She stepped across the threshold, her breath white in the chilled air.

"If you've got enough time to clean the shop this morning, that must mean you're planning on heading into school afterward?" she said, her hands on her hips.

"Well . . . But I—"

"But nothing! If you have nothing better to do, then come to school. Are you really planning to miss the rest of your classes before you move?"

"Yeah, I guess so."

Sayo gave the stammering boy a dangerous look.

"Hey, think about how I feel—I'm the one at my depressed classmate's house, dropping off homework. I'm trying to be nice."

Rintaro realized he'd never thanked her for bringing his homework by the day before. But as soon as he mumbled, "Thank you for yesterday," Sayo got a puzzled expression on her face.

"Did I say something wrong?" asked Rintaro.

"No, I'm just surprised. You didn't look happy at all about it yesterday, and now you're standing here, thanking me to my face."

"I wasn't unhappy about it. You're the one who looked pissed . . ."

"Pissed?"

Sayo was taken aback for a moment, but then added: "Not especially."

But now she did look a little mad.

"I was just worried about you, Natsuki."

"Worried? About me?" Rintaro said, surprised.

"Of course."

Sayo looked sharply at him.

"Your grandfather dies, and now you have to move away—I got all worried about you. But *then* I find you just hanging out with Akiba like everything's fine. That really bugged me."

I hadn't realized, thought Rintaro. Selfishly, he had thought that Sayo had been coming by out of duty. Even though she had told him straight out that she was worried about him, he assumed she had just said it out of politeness. But it seemed that wasn't the case.

One moment Sayo was staring at him in amazement, then suddenly, she looked away.

"Did I really look pissed?" Sayo asked.

Rintaro was lost for words. It wasn't because of her question—it was because, despite seeing Sayo hundreds of times, he'd never noticed before how bright and beautiful her eyes were. When he thought about it, he realized that she lived right around the corner, but he'd never had a face-to-face conversation with her before.

"What, did I seem like that big of a jerk?"

". . . I didn't think that at all."

"You're a really bad liar, Natsuki."

Rintaro had no answer for that. He reached up with his right hand and fiddled with his glasses for a moment.

"I've got Grandpa's old tea set," he said finally, pointing awkwardly toward the back of the shop. "If you have time, I could make you a cup."

Ugh, thought Rintaro. What a stupid line that was. His clumsy invitation was met with a mild grimace from his cheerful classmate.

"What's that? A pickup line?" Sayo asked.

"Of course not!"

"But as an invitation to someone who came all the way here to bring you your homework, it's not bad."

It was a slick response. She moved over and plopped down on the stool next to Rintaro.

"I'm going to give you points for effort," she said.

"Thanks for that."

Rintaro barely had time to sigh with relief before Sayo continued, "I'll have a cup of Darjeeling with plenty of sugar."

Her upbeat voice was like the unexpected arrival of spring in the midst of winter.

THE SECOND LABYRINTH

The Mutilator
of Books

Rintaro's grandfather had always been a mysterious character.

He seemed to inhabit a slightly different reality than the one Rintaro knew. A man of few words, elusive, but not standoffish or cold. He came across as a quiet, wise old man.

He would get up at 6:00 a.m. and finish breakfast by half past. By 7:00 a.m. he would have prepared bento lunch boxes for both Rintaro and himself. Then he'd open the doors and windows to air out the shop and water the outside plants. From morning time when he saw his grandson off to school, to the early evening when Rintaro returned, he never surfaced from his ocean of secondhand books. His daily routine was regular, unchanging, like a river flowing steadily to the sea.

You would imagine this little old man had lived his whole life in that bookshop, but that couldn't have been further from the truth.

Rintaro's grandfather didn't talk about it much, but he had once held a rather important post at a university somewhere. Rintaro heard from one of the elderly customers that he'd suffered some kind of a breakdown. The man who confided this to him was a silver-bearded gentleman who always turned up at the shop dressed in a suit with a bolo tie. He'd drop by from time to time to purchase some thick work of literature, or occasionally foreign language books. He told Rintaro that he used to be a colleague of his grandfather's.

"Your grandpa is a wonderful human being," he once told Rintaro, reaching down and ruffling the boy's hair.

That must have been when Rintaro was still in junior high school. Grandpa had been out on an errand, leaving his grandson in charge of the shop.

"He took some of the world's most troubling problems and did everything he could to try to find a solution. He made the greatest of efforts, dedicated his whole mind to them. He did seriously brilliant work."

The silver-haired man absentmindedly stroked the exquisite, cross-shaped design on the cover of a book as he reminisced.

"But—"

The man broke off. He sighed as he scanned the bookshelves in front of him.

"It wasn't enough. He retired from the world stage before accomplishing his goal."

World stage? Rintaro didn't associate that kind of phrase with his grandfather at all.

"What was my grandpa trying to accomplish?" Rintaro asked. The old man smiled.

"Nothing exceptional. He just tried to remind people of the obvious. Not to tell lies. Never bully someone weaker than themselves. To help out those in need . . ."

Rintaro looked confused. The old man grimaced slightly.

"Because the obvious is no longer obvious in today's world."

He gave a deeper sigh, then continued.

"In today's world, a lot of what should be obvious has been turned upside down. The weak are used as stepping-stones and those in need are taken advantage of. People just get caught up in this pattern. Nobody stands up and calls for it to stop."

"But my grandfather did?" Rintaro asked.

"Yes. He said stop. He said it was wrong. He patiently kept trying to persuade people."

The old man continued to tell the boy how, despite his grandfather's efforts, nothing ever changed.

As if he were handling an elegant glass carving, he gently placed two heavy volumes onto the cash desk. They were James Boswell's *Life of Samuel Johnson.*

"Do you have the third volume, too?"

"We do. Up there to the left. Second shelf from the top. Probably next to the Voltaire."

The old man nodded and smiled. He went to the shelf and brought back the volume he'd been looking for.

"Are you saying that something happened to Grandpa's job at the university, so he ended up opening this bookshop instead?"

"Yes, I suppose that's the gist of it. But it wasn't quite like that."

Rintaro stared blankly at the man.

"Your grandfather didn't just give up or run away without putting up a fight." He laughed. "He simply changed his approach."

"Approach?"

"Your grandfather opened a wonderful secondhand bookshop. And by doing that he was able to get all kinds of amazing books into the hands of many people. He believed that way he might be able to begin to right some wrongs, straighten out some of the things that had gotten twisted. What I mean is, this was the path that he chose. Not exactly the most glorious of routes, but a gutsy choice—typical of your grandfather."

The old man paused from his earnest retelling and gave the boy a smile.

"Is this all a bit difficult for you to follow?"

It is, Rintaro thought.

Right at that moment, he couldn't grasp all the details, but it was as if he were seeing things a little differently. If you asked him what had changed, he wouldn't be able to explain. But somehow in the last few days, as he'd gotten into the regular rhythm of cleaning and maintaining, he'd gradually begun to understand the connection between his taciturn grandfather and this little shop, Natsuki Books.

Dusting the bookshelves and sweeping the front step was monotonous, repetitive work, and it took a surprising amount of time and effort. But it had helped him to understand how patient his grandfather had always been and how much care the old man had always taken.

Rintaro looked around the shop with affection. He was feeling a bit sentimental.

He'd spent an hour this morning cleaning and arranging the shop. Now strips of winter sunlight filtered through the slats of the lattice door and reflected off the wooden floorboards. The cheerful conversation he could hear outside was doubtless groups of high school students on their way to morning club activities. Their laughter was carried on the cold winter air. It really was the pleasantest of breezes.

"Slacking off again, Mr. Proprietor? What happened to school?"

It came out of nowhere, but this time Rintaro wasn't fazed by the familiar voice. He rested the handle of his duster on his shoulder and turned to look.

The furry tabby cat was sitting at the far end of the narrow aisle. The back wall had vanished once again and had been replaced by rows of bookshelves stretching on forever into the bluish light.

Rintaro grimaced.

"I'd like to welcome you with an '*irasshaimase*,' as I do my other customers, so could you come in by the front door for once? That way's supposed to be the back wall."

"You seem strangely unperturbed to see me, Mr. Proprietor," said the cat in its distinctive deep voice. Its jade eyes had that knowing gleam. "It'd be helpful if you reacted with a little more amazement. I would be much more amused."

"I've been thinking about how you called where we went 'the first labyrinth.' That means there's going to be a second one, right?"

"Such amazing powers of wisdom. Such penetrating insight! Guess that'll save me the trouble of explaining."

"Explaining what?"

"The second labyrinth. I need your help again."

"You're not . . . ?"

Rintaro glanced down the never-ending aisle of books.

"You're going to get me to help you rescue books again, aren't you?" he ventured.

The cat's reaction was grandiose and far from humble.

"Correct!"

━━━

"Somewhere there is a man who steadily acquires books from all over the world, then chops them up into tiny pieces," said the cat solemnly. "He collects books and then mistreats them horribly. We can't let him continue to get away with it."

Rintaro sat down on the stool by the cash desk and began to fiddle with his glasses. He was silent for a while, observing the tabby at his feet.

"What?" the cat protested. "Do you think staring at my face is going to make things better? Are you coming with me or not?"

"You're pushier than ever."

"You'd never do anything unless I pushed you. And I can tell you my life's a lot easier if I don't have to be pushy."

The light in the green eyes seemed to get more intense. Rintaro thought it over a little while longer.

"Okay then."

He sighed deeply.

"So I just follow you again?"

The cat seemed taken aback by the simple response. It narrowed its eyes.

"What a refreshing attitude. I thought you were going to start squirming like a little worm again."

"Well, I may not properly understand difficult concepts, but one thing I learned from my grandpa was that you should always handle books with care. Helping people out may not be my forte, but when I hear that books need my help then I'm ready."

The cat's eyes widened a moment, then narrowed once more.

"Fine then."

There may have been the hint of a smile, but before Rintaro could really register it, they were interrupted by the jingle of the doorbell. He turned to see a face peering in through the doorway.

"You alive, Natsuki?"

It was the peppy voice of class rep Sayo Yuzuki. Rintaro glanced at the clock and saw it was 7:30 a.m. She must have been on her way to morning band practice again. Rintaro went into a panic.

"Who's this? Your girlfriend?" said the cat.

"Be quiet!" Rintaro hissed.

It was only two days since Sayo and Rintaro had tea together. Rintaro had only replied vaguely to her pleas for him to go back to school, and ever since he had stayed holed up inside Natsuki Books. Really there didn't seem any reason to go to school at all at this point. But he always wavered whenever Sayo was there in front of him.

And in what was already such a delicate situation, for her to come and try to persuade him first thing in the morning while he was talking to a cat . . . Well, it was awkward, to say the least.

"Wh— What's up?"

"Nothing's up."

Frowning slightly, Sayo made her way uninvited into the shop. Rintaro heard the cat's voice whispering in his ear.

"Don't worry, Mr. Proprietor. Only certain people are able to see me, and only under special conditions. Just act like I'm not here."

Rintaro was skeptical, but there was nothing to be done.

"You didn't turn up the other day, and it looks like you're not coming today, either," Sayo said.

"No. That's not . . ."

"So you're coming to school?"

"Today? Yeah, I haven't—"

Seeing Rintaro was in peak waffling mode, Sayo glared at him.

"If you take another day off, I'll have to bring your homework by *again*. The teachers are really worried about you, too. Do you realize how much stress you're causing for everyone?"

As usual, she wasn't holding back. She already had so much more dignity than Rintaro would ever have.

"Sorry," Rintaro said.

"This isn't about saying sorry. If you plan to come, then come. If you want to skip, just skip. I know your situation's really tough right now. But if you keep wimping out on making any kind of decision, nobody will be able to help you."

Sayo's rapid-fire delivery style only made Rintaro feel worse. He'd believed that he was so unimportant, such a nobody, that his absence from school would go unnoticed, but the look in his class rep's eyes told a different story.

A laugh came from just behind him.

"She's spot-on. People are really worried about you. You clearly have more friends than you care to admit."

The tabby seemed to be enjoying itself a little too much, so Rintaro turned and flashed it a look. It paid him no attention, its furry coat shaking with laughter.

But to Rintaro's alarm, Sayo let out a short gasp and looked down in the direction of his feet. Of course, that was where the poison-tongued tabby cat was sitting.

The cat froze, and there followed an extremely uncomfortable silence.

"Can you actually see me?" it asked Sayo, in a voice tinged with wonder. "And hear my voice, too?"

"A talking cat?"

The tabby started in shock. Sayo was looking straight at it. She then shifted her gaze to the faint blue light at the far end of the bookshop.

"Wh . . . What's that?"

Rintaro followed her gaze. His hand slowly moved up to his glasses.

"Didn't you mention something about certain people and special conditions?"

"Yes, that was supposed to be the case."

The cat was unusually flustered.

"Well, this is a bit of a mess."

"Natsuki?" said Sayo. "I'm seeing something really weird."

"Well, that's a relief. I thought it was just me."

Rintaro's casual response left Sayo speechless.

The cat, however, had already regained its usual composure. It padded its way over to Sayo and gave a deep bow.

"I'm Tiger the Tabby."

There was surprising grace in its movement.

"Nice to meet you."

The girl still seemed confused, but then in the next instant she reached out and scooped the cat up into her arms.

"So cute!"

Both Rintaro and the cat froze.

"What an adorable tabby cat! And how cool that it can talk!"

"Are you okay with this?" whispered Rintaro to his feline friend.

Sayo was quite taken with the cat and her delighted voice filled the shop. The cat, finding itself squished cheek to cheek with the girl, began meowing helplessly.

"So now you meow?" said Rintaro, with a sigh of defeat.

Girl, boy, and cat made their way down the center aisle with its giant towering bookcases on either side. The tabby took the lead, followed by Sayo, and Rintaro took up the rear. The cat stepped silently, Sayo had a light spring to her step, but Rintaro practically trudged.

"Sayo, you really ought to turn back."

Sayo turned and glowered at Rintaro.

"What? So you're the only one who can go on fantastic adventures with a talking cat?"

"Fantastic adventures . . . ?"

Rintaro tried again—this time with a little more trepidation.

"There's no need for you to get involved in this stuff. It's dangerous."

"'Dangerous'?"

Sayo gave Rintaro a hard look.

"So, Natsuki, you're telling me to shut up and let a class-mate keep putting himself in danger?"

"Well, no. That wasn't what I meant . . ."

"Which is it? If it's not dangerous, then it should be no problem for me to go with you. If it is dangerous, then it wouldn't be a good idea for me to let you walk into it alone. Am I right?"

The phrase "straight as an arrow" was coined to describe Sayo Yuzuki, Rintaro thought. He admired her. Compared with the procrastinating, wishy-washy worrier that was Rintaro, Sayo's argument was clear and persuasive. A weakling of a shut-in like himself couldn't even try to oppose her.

"Give it up, Mr. Proprietor," the cat interceded. "Whichever way you look at it, you're going to lose the battle."

"I admit I'm in the weaker position, but I don't need to hear it from you, seeing as you're the cause of the whole problem," Rintaro said.

"Well, I guess you could say that. But she saw me. What can you do?"

The cat was throwing out its usual quick responses, but it didn't have quite the same energy in its voice as before. It was still rather shaken by what had transpired.

"I can't see into the future," it continued. "I would never have guessed this would happen."

"You always act as if you know what you're doing, but in fact you're just winging it, aren't you?" Rintaro said.

"You were outsmarted by me, Natsuki," Sayo butted in. "Don't take it out on the poor kitty."

"What are you talking about? 'Take it out on'?"

"Well, aren't you?"

"I'm worried about getting my class rep mixed up in this bizarre thing. I feel responsible, that's all."

"Of course it'd be a big problem if anything happened to me. But it'd be the same if anything happened to you, too, right, Natsuki?"

There was quick-wittedness buried in her seemingly casual tone. Seeing Rintaro tongue-tied, Sayo continued her verbal assault.

"You know, your personality's not *all* bad, Natsuki, but I really can't stand this part of it."

And with that, she picked up the pace, bravely following the cat farther down the long passageway—the antithesis of Rintaro, for whom every action was done in fear.

The cat came over to him and cocked its head to look up at his face.

"Young love!"

"What are you talking about?"

Just as Rintaro managed to mumble his question, the party finally entered the perimeter of a bright white light.

A hospital?

That was Rintaro's first thought.

They'd emerged from the dazzling light into a wide-open space filled with men and women in white coats, rushing about to and fro. But as the dazzle of the light faded away and the space came properly into view, its bizarreness became clearer.

Ahead of them was a giant stone walkway. The width was about that of two school classrooms, and the depth seemed to go on forever. To either side, a line of mighty, elegant pillars, evenly spaced, supported a grand arched roof. If you took in only these pillars, the view resembled an ancient Greek temple, but there was something very odd about the people coming and going. They appeared from between the pillars on one side, then disappeared between the ones on the opposite side. There were both men and women of a wide range of ages, but each was dressed in white and carried a pile of books in their hands. Their movements were identical.

On the wall between each pillar, there were shelves of books reaching way up to the high vaulted ceiling. At regular intervals at the foot of the walls that made up this giant library, there was a large desk. Teams of workers were busily searching for books on the shelves and piling them up on the desks. Next, they would pick up different books from the desk and return them to the shelves. If you looked carefully, you could see that there was a series of narrow pathways cut into the wall, and staircases leading up and down. The people would emerge from these pathways, stop in front of one of the desks to drop off and pick up books, cross over the giant walkway, and disappear once more into one of the passageways on the other side of the room.

It was a hectic, dizzying scene—people scurrying around clutching piles of books, others carefully piling books onto desks, and yet others working at the top of a tall ladder.

"Look at this . . . this place is amazing!"

Sayo was always frank about her feelings. As she stared wide-eyed around the space, a woman hurried right by her. No one paid the least attention to the two teens and a cat. It was as if they hadn't even noticed them, and yet, if a collision was imminent, they would dodge and pass around the three intruders. So it wasn't that they couldn't see . . . But the most curious thing of all was that there were so many of these people running around the place, and yet not a single word of conversation to be heard. It was like watching a badly made silent movie.

"So somewhere in here there's a person cutting up books?" asked Rintaro.

"That's what I heard."

"What are we going to do?"

The cat shrugged.

"Look for him?"

The cat quickly approached the nearest of the men and called out to him.

"Excuse me. I'd like to ask you something."

The man stopped in his tracks, a tall pile of books in his arms. He looked down at the tabby cat with obvious irritation. He was middle-aged, well-built, but his complexion was oddly pale.

"What is it? I'm busy!"

"What the hell is this place?" asked the cat.

The cat's tone was scornful, but the man's reply was matter-of-fact.

"This is the Institute of Reading Research. We're the world's largest research facility dedicated to all aspects of reading."

"Reading research?" Sayo asked.

The man ignored her furrowed brow.

"Then I'd like to meet the person in charge," the cat said.

"Person in charge?"

"Right. The head of this facility. The director. Or if you're calling it a 'research institute,' maybe I should call them the doctor or professor?"

"You're looking for a professor?"

"Yep."

"Give it up," said the man without even blinking. "There are as many people in the world with the title of professor as there are stars in the sky. Japan is full of professors. Try it— shout out 'Professor!' right now. Four out of every five of the scholars in this room will turn around. They're all professors with their own particular field of research. There are thousands of them here—experts in speed-reading to stenography. There are always brand-new professors turning up in all sorts of fields—rhetoric, syntax, style, phonology; studying character fonts, paper quality—you name it, this place is overflowing with them. Here, you'd have a lot more luck finding someone who isn't a professor."

The cat looked disappointed at the man's response, and the latter took advantage of the moment of silence to bid them goodbye and be on his way.

"Hey!" the cat called after him, but he was already disappearing into one of the passageways behind a pillar. Rintaro and Sayo just stared blankly after him.

"What the hell was that?"

The cat ignored Rintaro and set off again along the giant walkway, stopping the next man to cross its path. He was a different age and build to the previous one, but had the same bloodless complexion and was carrying a similar pile of books.

"What is it? I'm really busy."

"We're looking for someone."

"You'd better not," the man shot back. "This is a vast research facility, full of people who look alike, think alike, and are all likewise busy. Of course, everyone is eager to assert their own uniqueness, but since everyone is equally obsessed with asserting it, then there's nothing unique about anyone. It turns out it's impossible to distinguish between us. In a place like this, trying to find a particular 'someone' is not only difficult, it's meaningless. Goodbye."

And with that, he was gone.

Next the cat spoke to a relatively young woman, but her

washed-out complexion and mystifying reply was just like those of the previous two men.

Right as they were looking around for a fourth person to ask, Sayo collided with a young man. He lost his grip on his pile of books and they spilled to the floor.

"I'm so sorry," she said, bowing. The man threw her a look of contempt and quickly began to gather up his books. Rintaro began to help him, but suddenly came to a halt, a book in his hand.

Recommendations for a Whole New Way of Reading.

Whatever way he looked at it, it was a poor title for a book.

"Where is the person who wrote this book?" he asked.

The man raised an eyebrow and stared at Rintaro.

"We're looking for the man who wrote this book," Rintaro repeated.

"If you're looking for the director, go down those stairs to the Director's Office. You'll find him there."

His arms full of books once more, he flicked his chin in the direction of one of the pillars to the right of the room. Behind it was a tiny set of stairs leading downward.

"The director's so devoted to his research that he locks himself down there in his office and rarely comes up to ground level. If you go down there, you're bound to meet him."

Somehow, his reply managed to be pompous without showing the slightest emotion.

"Thank you," said Rintaro, bowing. But by the time he'd

lifted his head, the man had already disappeared up a staircase on the opposite side of the hall.

They set off down the staircase but soon realized it didn't have an end.

"So this is why he rarely sets foot on ground level," grumbled Sayo.

Her voice was immediately sucked down and echoed dully somewhere deep below them.

"Do you think it's okay to keep going?"

"If you don't like it, you can always go home," replied Rintaro. "You know I've always been the kind of guy to recommend going home."

"All right then, everyone in favor of going home, be my guest. Turn right around. As for me, I'm in the 'once you've started something you never give up halfway through' school of thought."

Sayo's words seemed to brighten the gloom of their surroundings. Rintaro immediately fell silent.

The stairs that had begun by leading straight down gradually began to curve and spiral. Dark and murky in every direction, it felt as if they were being pulled down into the profoundest depths of the earth. The view was unchanging. The staircase walls were lit at intervals with lamps, in between which there were random piles of books. Some were brand new, others older, but what they all had in common was their title: *Recommendations for a Whole New Way of Reading.* From time to time, men in white coats would pass them, coming up the stairs with an armful of books, but they would hurry on by, paying the trio absolutely no heed.

All of a sudden Sayo cried out.

"Beethoven?"

Rintaro stopped to listen. It was true—faint music was filtering up from far below.

"It's Beethoven's Symphony Number Nine, the third movement I think."

"Beethoven's Ninth?" Rintaro said.

The vice captain of the wind ensemble club nodded confidently.

As they continued downward, the music became louder, and Rintaro could clearly make out the refined melody of the string section.

"The second theme."

Right as Sayo called it, the melody changed, and a more expansive, slower theme began. The three adventurers seemed to be pulled in by the swell of strings and wind instruments, and their pace visibly quickened. In an instant they found themselves at the bottom of the staircase in front of a modest wooden door. Above the door was a nameplate that said "Director's Office." There was no other adornment or marking of any kind. From inside came orchestral music at a high volume. It wasn't the most appealing sight, but the group were just relieved to have finally reached the end of that interminable staircase.

At a nod from the cat, Rintaro knocked softly on the door.

He knocked twice, and then a third time, much harder, but there was no response besides the sound of Beethoven's Ninth.

Hesitantly, Rintaro took hold of the door handle and pushed.

With a faint creak, the door swung open, and a blast of terrifyingly loud music assaulted the trio.

The room was not particularly large. Well, it was hard to guess its actual size due to the piles of books and papers stacked up to the ceiling on all four sides. The space between all the books was rather narrow, with a single desk in the middle, facing away from the door. The desk, too, was buried under mounds of paper.

Sitting at the desk, his back to Rintaro and the others, was a man, not tall, but rather heavily built. He was completely absorbed in some kind of work. Rintaro could make out that he was holding a book in his left hand; in his right, a pair of scissors. To everyone's shock, he appeared to be chopping up the book. With every movement of the scissors, pieces of paper flew into the air and the book became less and less booklike.

The sight of this broad man in a white coat, immersed in such a bizarre task, was curious to say the least.

"What the . . ."

Sayo was at a loss for words. Even the tabby cat could do nothing but stare.

Of course, the blasting sound of the Ninth Symphony only added to the weirdness of the scene. It was coming from a machine next to him on the desk. It was neither a CD nor a record player—Rintaro recognized it as an old-style cassette tape player, the kind of boom box that had seen its heyday at least a generation earlier. The only reason he recognized it was because his grandfather had owned one. There was something faintly ridiculous about the sight of the tiny spinning wheels of the cassette tape.

"Excuse me," ventured Rintaro, but the man didn't move. He tried again, but there was still no reaction. He took a deep breath and produced his loudest possible voice from deep in his belly. At last the man stopped what he was doing and turned around.

"Yes? What is it?" he said in a high-pitched voice.

The man had a very peculiar appearance. He wore thick glasses, his white coat was heavily wrinkled over his protruding belly, and his head was bald, save for a few stray gray hairs. The wearing of a lab coat seemed to suggest that he was some sort of scholar or researcher, but other than that there wasn't a hint of anything intellectual or educated about him.

"We're very sorry to bother you," continued Rintaro.

"Oh, yeah—sorry about that," yelled the man, loudly enough to be heard over the strident tones of Beethoven's Ninth. "Didn't notice you come in."

As he spun his chair around to face his visitors, both Sayo and Rintaro flinched at the sight of a pair of scissors in one hand and a mangled book in the other.

"Rarely get any guests here," he explained. "So sorry there's nowhere to sit."

His voice continued to boom over the top of the music.

"What do you want?"

Rintaro raised his voice to match.

"We came because we heard that books were being cut to pieces. Are you—"

"Huh? What's that?"

"We heard a lot of books were being cut up—"

"Sorry, I can't hear you. Could you speak up a bit?"

"I said, lots of books were—"

All of a sudden there was a painfully shrill noise, and the music came to an abrupt end. In its place a chilling silence filled the room. The man frowned and struggled out of his chair, reaching out toward the boom box on the edge of his desk.

"Er . . ." At Rintaro's interruption the man froze, his pudgy hand still in midair.

"Your tape and the cassette player are pretty old. Sometimes the tape gets tangled up inside."

The man clicked the button to open the machine and began to extract the cassette tape. If you listened to an ancient cassette tape over and over again, it was bound to get loose and eventually get caught up in the mechanism. It must have been a common occurrence for him, because with utter calm he removed the tape from the player, carefully wound it tight again, and replaced it in the player. Then he clicked the play button again. Not two seconds later, the thunderous sounds of Beethoven's Ninth started up again.

"Tell me again what it is you want," yelled the man.

Rintaro frowned at the booming scholar.

"Don't look at me like that," he said. "Beethoven is one of my favorite composers—I especially admire his Ninth Symphony. My research always goes so much better when I listen to him."

"Research? What research?" Rintaro spat out with disgust, but the middle-aged man didn't seem to notice. On the contrary he nodded with delight.

"I'm very glad you asked. The focus of my research is, in short, 'The Streamlining of Reading.'"

"You know what?" whispered Sayo in Rintaro's ear. "I think that he's using Beethoven to block out all the stuff he doesn't want to hear."

That may very well have been true, but there was nothing they could do about it. For now, Rintaro grabbed at the thread that had been dangled before him.

"What do you mean by the streamlining of reading?"

"Well, that's simple. In short, research into how to read faster."

The scholar grinned and made chopping motions with his scissors.

"There are so many books in the world, but we humans are so busy that we can never find the time to read them all. But when my research is complete, people will be able to read several dozen books every day. And not only the most popular bestsellers—but also complex stories and even difficult philosophical works. This is going to be one of the greatest accomplishments in the history of mankind."

"Dozens of books a day?"

"Are you talking about speed-reading?"

Rintaro and Sayo responded simultaneously.

The scholar nodded happily.

"Speed-reading is a very important skill. But in general speed-reading doesn't work unless you're familiar with the kind of text you're reading. For example, it's extremely useful for picking out the information you need from a list of stock prices in a newspaper, but someone new to philosophy isn't going to be able to speed-read Husserl's *Ideas Pertaining to a Pure Phenomenology* just like that. Now—"

A self-satisfied smile on his face, he added a dramatic pause and raised a thick forefinger in the air.

"I have been successful in combining a second skill with speed-reading."

"A second skill?"

"That of summary!"

Rintaro and Sayo could barely believe what they were hearing.

The moment was punctuated by the end of the symphony's third movement. There was a fleeting silence and then the fourth movement began with its intense cacophony of wind instruments. The scholar raised his voice even louder.

"Summary, synopsis—call it what you will. Those who have mastered speed-reading can even further increase their speed by the use of extracts from the text, known as a 'summary' or 'synopsis.' Of course, we eliminate all technical terms and jargon, unique or stylish phrases or expressions, or any rich or subtle idioms. The style is free from any individuality, expressions are deliberately kept to those in common usage—the passages are touched up to achieve the utmost plainness and simplicity. In this way, a story that used to take, say, ten minutes to read can now be polished off in under a minute."

The scholar reached down to pick up a book that had fallen on the floor. Randomly inserting his scissors, he snipped off a fragment of a page, then leaned forward to show it to Rintaro.

There was a single line of text. Rintaro read it aloud:

"Melos was furious."

The scholar nodded contentedly.

"That's the summary of 'Run, Melos!' by Osamu Dazai."

Rintaro was dumbstruck. Meanwhile, the man began to wave around what remained of the text.

"You see, even a famous short story like this one can be summarized. All it needs is this sentence. I performed extraction after extraction and ended up with this sentence. Naturally, if you use my streamlining method, you'll be able to read the whole of 'Run, Melos!' in 0.5 seconds. Novels and other longer books pose more of a problem."

He stretched a fleshy arm toward the boom box and turned the volume up even louder. "Ode to Joy" played by the lower stringed instruments echoed exuberantly through the room.

"I'm currently working on Goethe's *Faust*. The goal is to get it down to two minutes, but it's proving to be quite a challenge."

He slapped a pile of books on his desk. The force caused several of the snippets of paper lying around to dance like snowflakes. It was impossible to tell if any of these books were copies of *Faust*, because they had seemingly all already undergone the scissors treatment.

"I've already succeeded in eliminating 90 percent of the book, but even at 10 percent of the original, this is still a huge project. It really needs to be condensed further. It's going to take a lot of work. But there are many people who wish to read *Faust*, so I need to meet their expectations."

The only reason that Rintaro didn't come right out with "Are you crazy?" was because Sayo managed to get there first.

"Isn't that a weird way to go about it?" She spoke up, but her voice was unfortunately overpowered somewhat by the sound of Beethoven.

"Weird? Why?" the scholar asked.

"Well . . ."

The directness of the question threw her for a moment. The scholar was halfway through turning his chair back toward his desk, but now he swung back around to face his visitors full on.

"They say that people don't read anymore. But that's just not true. They're too busy. There really is a limit to the time they can spend on reading. But there are so many books they want to read. People naturally want to be exposed to lots of different stories. Want to read *The Brothers Karamazov* or *The Grapes of Wrath*? How should we fulfill that need?"

The scholar stuck out his double chin.

"Speed-reading and a synopsis. That's how."

He hadn't touched the cassette player, but somehow the volume of the Ninth Symphony seemed to swell up even further.

"This book here . . ."

From the pile of paper scraps to his right, the scholar produced an ancient-looking book. It was the same title the trio had seen over and over on their journey down to the director's office: *Recommendations for a Whole New Way of Reading*.

"This is my masterpiece, a compilation of all my research. Here, along with the latest speed-reading techniques, are the synopses of a hundred classic books, from both Eastern and Western cultures, that I have devoted myself to summarizing. In other words, if you have this book on your shelf, you'll be able to read a hundred books in a single day. I have a second and third volume in the works. Very soon, people will have access to books from all over the world without wasting even the tiniest bit of time. Isn't that wonderful?"

"I see," said Rintaro. Of course, he didn't really see at all, but he felt he needed to say something in order to stop the man going on forever.

"Even so, what you're reading is something entirely different from the original book," Rintaro added.

"Different? Well, I suppose it may have been changed a bit."

"Not only a bit." The tabby cat's deep voice resounded through the room. "By doing this, collecting all these books and chopping them to bits, all you're doing is mutilating them, reducing them to scraps of paper. What that means is you're robbing the book of any life."

"You're wrong!"

The man's voice tore at them like a great gust of wind. There was a weight to his tone that hadn't been there before.

"I'm breathing new life into these books. Look . . ."

His tone switched again; this time he spoke with gentle admonishment.

"If stories aren't read, they're going to disappear. I'm just lending a hand to help keep them alive. I summarize them. I provide a means to speed-read. That way, lost stories can leave their mark on the present day, and at the same time people who want to engage with one of those stories, but only have so much time to spare, can do so."

He rose slowly to his feet, brandishing the scissors in his right hand like an orchestra conductor with a baton.

"*Melos was furious.* Don't you think that's the perfect summary?"

He set about his own imaginary conducting of Beethoven's symphony.

"Books and music are so similar, don't you think? They bring wisdom, courage, and healing to our lives. Created by human beings as tools that bring comfort and inspiration to ourselves. And yet, there is a major difference between the two."

As the rotund form of the scholar twisted and twirled to the multilayered melody, his white coat drew an exaggerated arc in the air, and the scissors flashed dangerously as they caught the light.

"Music can reach us every day in a variety of situations: your car stereo while driving, earbuds while you're out jogging, my cassette radio here in the lab. It can be heard by you anywhere, anytime, whatever you're doing. But not a book. You can listen to music while you're jogging, but you can't read a book. You can work on your research while listening to Beethoven's Ninth, but you can't write a paper and read *Faust* at the same time. Those pathetic limitations are why books are dying out. I'm dedicating myself to this research in order to rescue the book from its pitiful fate. I'm not mutilating these books. I'm saving them."

At the very moment he finished speaking, a baritone began to sing, almost as if the scholar had timed his speech to coincide with the music.

The cat didn't respond. Rintaro, for his part, could sort of understand what the man was saying. The same was true of the hoarder of books whom he had met on his previous adventure. Their approaches toward reading hinted at madness, but something about their words stung, preventing you from laughing. Perhaps it was the sting of truth.

"These days," said the scholar mildly, almost as if he had sensed the turmoil in Rintaro's heart, "a book isn't considered worthy just because it's profound or difficult. People want to enjoy masterpieces in an uncomplicated way, pleasurably, fashionably, as if they were a downloadable collection of Christmas songs. A masterpiece cannot survive if it doesn't adapt to the demands of the times. And so, I wield these scissors to sustain the life of such books."

"Mr. Proprietor?"

The voice of the cat brought Rintaro back to his senses.

"You're not impressed by all this, are you?"

"To be honest, I'm a little bit impressed."

"What the—!" The tabby cat glared at Rintaro, its whiskers stiffening in annoyance.

On the periphery of Rintaro's vision, the scholar was still waving his hands around, conducting an imaginary orchestra in his head. The overhead fluorescent light reflected in the scissors, and the "Ode to Joy," which had started out with a solo voice, had reached its first chorus.

"I admit it would be awesome to be able to read *Faust* in two minutes, but—"

"It's a fallacy. He's nothing but a sophist."

"Whether it's a fallacy or not," interrupted Sayo. "I kind of get what he means. I've always been a slow reader, and I'm not good with difficult books, so I'd be tempted to choose one that is easier to read, whether by speed-reading or a summary."

"You get it," announced the scholar with a good deal of satisfaction. "You really get it. And I want to be of use to people like you."

Sayo seemed bewitched. The normally intelligent and vivacious high school girl looked at the scholar with a dreamy expression, as if she were in some sort of trance.

The cat raised its voice, urgently.

"She's about to fall under his spell— Do something!"

"I don't know what to do!"

The loud tones of the "Ode to Joy" were too distracting for Rintaro to think clearly. The music had become a fence surrounding the scholar, keeping his visitors at bay.

Rintaro wiped the sweat from his forehead, then closed

his eyes, and lifted his right hand to his glasses frame. What would Grandpa have said in this situation?

He did his best to summon an image of his grandfather in his mind—the old man sitting in profile, lost in thought with his teacup tilted toward his mouth. His gentle eyes following the words on the page, his reading glasses glinting in the lamplight. Wrinkled fingers gently turning pages . . .

"Do you like the mountains, Rintaro?"

It seemed to come from somewhere deep inside Rintaro's own head; the rich voice of his grandfather as he carefully prepared a pot of tea.

"The mountains, Rintaro."

"I don't know. I've never climbed one."

Rintaro hadn't bothered to answer properly, probably too engrossed in the book he was reading. His grandfather had smiled and sat down beside his grandson.

"Reading a book is a lot like climbing a mountain."

"What do you mean?"

His curiosity piqued, Rintaro had finally looked up from his book. His grandfather wafted his teacup slowly under his nose as if savoring the aroma of the tea.

"Reading isn't only for pleasure or entertainment. Sometimes you need to examine the same lines deeply, read the same sentences over again. Sometimes you sit there, head in hands, only progressing at a painstakingly slow pace. And the result of all this hard work and careful study is that suddenly you're there and your field of vision expands. It's like finding a great view at the end of a long climbing trail."

Under the light of the old-fashioned lamp, Rintaro's grandfather sipped at his tea, calm and self-assured, and looking just like the wise old wizard in some fantasy novel.

"Reading can be grueling."

The old man's eyes twinkled behind his reading glasses.

"Of course it's good to enjoy reading. But the views you can see hiking on a light, pleasant walking trail are limited. Don't condemn the mountain because its trails are steep. It's also a valuable and enjoyable part of climbing to struggle up a mountain step by step."

He reached out one thin, bony hand and placed it on the boy's head.

"If you're going to climb, make it a tall mountain. The view will be so much better."

The voice was warm and comforting.

It surprised Rintaro that he had had such a conversation with his grandfather.

"Mr. Proprietor?"

At the sound of the tabby's voice, Rintaro's eyes flew open.

The first thing he noticed was that there was an obvious change in Sayo's appearance. Her cheeks had lost their healthy glow, and her sparkling eyes, emptied of all vitality, were no more than reflections of the pallid neon lighting. The strange paleness of her complexion now matched the faces of the white-coated workers they'd seen on their way here.

The symphony was reaching its climax, and as if being sucked into the music, Sayo began to walk toward the scholar. Instinctively, Rintaro reached out and grabbed her hand and pulled her back. Her hand was ice cold, and her slight frame put up no resistance. It was horrifying. Rintaro winced at her frigid skin, but didn't let go of her hand until he'd managed to lead her to a chair and sit her down.

"That's not going to buy you much time, Mr. Proprietor."

"I know."

Rintaro seemed unfazed by the warning. He had neither the majesty of the tabby cat, nor the wit of his friend Sayo, but in his dull uneventful life he had come across his fair share of crazy predicaments and crises.

The white-coated scholar in the middle of the room was still brandishing the scissors in his right hand, book in his left, as if conducting the music. Each time both hands came together, snippets of white paper flew through the air.

Rintaro knew nothing of "The Streamlining of Reading." However, it was obvious to him that speed-reading or reducing a book to a synopsis would completely take away its power. In the end, chopped-up sentences were nothing more than fragments.

Hurrying means that you miss out on many things. Riding a train will take you far, but it's a misconception to think that this will give you more insight. Flowers in the hedgerow and birds in the treetops are accessible only to the person who walks on their own two feet. Rintaro pondered all this before stepping toward the scholar.

He took his time, didn't rush, made no hasty decisions. He reached out with his right hand toward the cassette player on the desktop. Immediately, the scholar's pudgy hand shot out and grabbed Rintaro by the sleeve.

"Please don't turn off my music."

"I'm not going to turn it off."

Rintaro's amicable tone seemed to confuse the scholar, and Rintaro was able to reach out and press the fast-forward button.

There was a whirring sound and Beethoven's Ninth came tumbling out at three times the speed. A headlong, breakneck, and rather unsettling "Ode to Joy."

"Stop that! You're ruining it!"

"I totally agree," said Rintaro quietly. His finger never left the fast-forward button and the cacophony continued. "But if I fast-forward, you'll be able to get so much more out of your beloved Ninth Symphony."

The scholar was about to reply but he suddenly raised his eyebrows and swallowed his words.

"However," Rintaro went on, "it also means the music will be ruined. The Ninth Symphony has to be played at the Ninth Symphony's pace—if you want to listen to it properly."

Rintaro took his finger off the button. The chorus resumed its majestic song.

"This is the speed at which this song should be heard. Fast-forwarding sucks."

The chorus shifted one octave higher. *Freude! Freude!* they sang in rapturous joy.

The scholar looked at Rintaro.

"Books, too . . ."

His mumbled words were barely audible over the music.

"You're saying that they're the same?"

"I'm saying that speed-reading and quick summarizing is just like listening to the finale of this symphony on fast-forward," Rintaro said.

"The finale on fast-forward . . . ?"

"What I mean is, it might be interesting and stuff, but that's not Beethoven's symphony. If you love Beethoven's Ninth, you'll understand—it's the same way that I love books."

The scholar froze in place, his scissors still clutched in his hand. He stayed a few moments in thought, then he turned his heavy-browed eye on Rintaro.

"But books that aren't read disappear."

"Yeah. It's a pity."

"But you're okay with that?"

"No, like I said, it's a pity. And I think it's just as much of a shame that 'Run, Melos!' has been compressed into one single sentence. In the same way that music is made up of more than notes, books are more than just words."

"But . . ."

Still clutching the scissors, the scholar let out a strangled voice.

"These days people have forgotten how to sit and read a book. Don't you think that synopses and speed-reading are what our modern society demands?"

"I don't know and I don't care."

At this unexpectedly aggressive response, the scholar's beady eyes widened.

"I simply love books."

Rintaro paused to look at his adversary.

"It doesn't matter how much society might demand it. I object to cutting up books."

At some point, the musical performance had come to an end. All that could be heard was the slight rattle of the cassette tape turning. Without the music dominating the air of the study, the strange mechanical sound echoed through the room. The scholar looked down at the desk.

"I love books, too," he mumbled.

Rintaro gave him a small nod. He felt no ill will for the man in front of him. No human being who genuinely hated books would have come up with a plan like this. And there were grains of truth mixed in with his words. He wanted to preserve books. He wanted them to reach as many people as possible. Someone who thought this way didn't hate books at all. However . . .

"And yet here you are shredding them!" Rintaro couldn't help himself. "And you're telling me you're a person who loves books?"

The scholar raised an eyebrow, before taking a deep sigh.

"I don't appreciate being spoken to that way."

With a hint of a smile, he raised his right hand. The scissors immediately vanished in a flash of light. Simultaneously, there was a great fluttering sound, as the scraps of paper that had been piled on the desk leapt up and began to dance through the air.

Startled, Rintaro backed up a few paces.

As more and more scraps of paper joined the dance, the view quickly became a paper blizzard. Rintaro watched as the whirling scraps and shreds began to overlap here and there, connecting with one another, before gradually taking on the form of complete books.

In the midst of it all stood the scholar, utterly dejected. Seeing how forlorn his adversary looked, Rintaro picked up a reconstituted book from the desktop and offered it to him. The scholar looked at the cover.

"'Run, Melos!' . . ."

"I like that story, too. Why don't you read it aloud to yourself once in a while? It'll take a while, but I'm sure you won't regret it."

The scholar took the slim volume and stared at it. Meanwhile, the paper snowstorm continued to gather momentum. Books were returning to their original form and slipping from the blizzard to settle into their places on the bookshelves. It was a magnificent sight; from plain simple paperbacks to opulent, leather-bound volumes—one after the other books were taking up their rightful places.

Rintaro had barely noticed, but the room began to fill with a soft light, and the notes of "Ode to Joy" began to play. He glanced at the boom box but the little wheels of the cassette tape were no longer turning. It was the scholar—he was humming.

Bobbing his head happily along to the music with "Run, Melos!" in hand, the scholar unbuttoned his white coat and casually tossed it onto the desk. The discarded coat became enveloped in the brightening light.

"My young guest," he addressed Rintaro with a smile as he pulled off his tie and tossed it after his coat. "I've had a delightful time. I wish you all the best for the future."

And with an amicable nod of the head, the scholar spun around and began to walk away. His retreating figure, along with its cheerful humming, was quickly swallowed up. The tune faded farther and farther away, until eventually everything melted into the light.

Sayo opened her eyes, and for a while, she didn't move a muscle. She checked out her surroundings, trying to make sense of where she was.

She'd been asleep in the corner of Natsuki Books. Apparently, she'd sat down on a wooden stool, leaned her head against a bookshelf, and fallen asleep. The blanket that had been placed over her and the little paraffin heater by her side showed that someone had taken care of her. There was a white kettle on top of the heater from which steam was gently rising.

She looked toward the front door of the shop, where morning sun was shining in. Standing with his back to the light, deep in thought, his hand fiddling with the frame of his glasses, was her classmate. There was something solemn about the way he was staring at the bookcases, as if burning every cover, every title onto his retinas, and engraving each of the stories within into his heart.

"You really do love books, don't you?"

At Sayo's words, Rintaro turned as if only just realizing she was there. He sighed with relief.

"Thank goodness. I was beginning to worry you were never going to wake up. You were out cold."

"I'm exhausted from all these morning practice sessions. But I have to tell you, I'm not in the habit of falling asleep at other people's houses."

Sayo's voice was livelier than ever, probably to cover up the fact that she was blushing. She continued hastily.

"Thanks, Natsuki. Looks like I was a bit of a pain."

"A pain?"

"You had to carry me back, right? From that strange place . . ."

Rintaro looked away for a moment, then shook his head rather deliberately.

"You must have had some weird dream."

"Hey!" Sayo's expression turned fierce. "Don't even think of pretending it was all a dream. That's not going to work, because I remember the whole thing. The talking cat, the passageway through the bookshelves, that crazy research facility. Shall I go on?"

"No, that's enough," said Rintaro, waving both hands to cut her off. "It's fine. I got it."

"Okay then." Sayo laughed.

In the back of her mind that mysterious scene kept resurfacing. Those people in the white coats rushing around, that endless staircase down into the ground, the booming sound of the Ninth Symphony, and the bizarre conversation. But then somewhere in the middle of that conversation, it all became fuzzy. As if she were sinking down into a deep, dark ocean. But she recalled how somewhere in the midst of it her classmate's warm hand had taken hers and pulled her back. How could that strong, reliable grip have belonged to this quiet, unassuming boy?

"What happened to the kitty-cat?"

Rintaro shook his head.

"I didn't see it on the way back. Just like the last time—it disappeared without saying goodbye."

"So does that mean it's possible we might meet it again?"

"You look pleased about it," Rintaro said, looking a little perplexed. "I was hoping not to get you mixed up in any more of these crazy happenings."

"I'm already plenty mixed up in it," Sayo quipped.

She got to her feet and stretched. Outside the door the light was fresh and vivid. According to the clock on the wall, hardly any time had passed since she had walked into the shop that morning. She'd apparently only just arrived. Everything seemed so normal that it was easy to believe it had been no more than a dream. Squinting a little in the bright sunlight, Sayo changed the subject.

"How's the moving prep going, Natsuki?"

"I haven't even started."

"Are you going to be okay?"

"Probably not," he said with a shrug. "I don't think I've accepted it yet."

"What do you mean? 'Accepted'?"

"I don't know how to explain it. Maybe I just don't want to leave this place . . . I think about it all the time, but I'm really having a hard time coming to terms with everything. Though I know I don't have time to be acting like this."

Sayo wanted to tell him that thinking wasn't going to help anything, but instead, she simply watched him. She felt strangely awkward. Rintaro was being vague as usual, but this time, what he was expressing felt like something besides mere indecision. He genuinely seemed to be trying to express all the mixed emotions pent up inside him. Sayo's eyes widened slightly as if she'd suddenly had an epiphany. Behind this boy's passiveness and unreliability, she'd just glimpsed something— someone totally earnest, honest to a fault.

Sayo's thoughts were interrupted by the carefree laughter of a group of high school girls passing by the shop. She turned to Rintaro and perked her own voice up to match theirs.

"How about you give me some book recommendations!"

Rintaro looked a little worried.

"Sure, but the kind of books I like are kind of heavy."

"Fine by me. It's not like I'm going to go looking for a synopsis after all that's happened."

Rintaro laughed.

"Glad to hear it."

He looked up at the shelves, his right hand on his glasses. Sayo was semishocked at how much his motionless profile reminded her of an old scholarly professor, filled with experience and good sense.

"Which one should we . . ."

Rintaro's habitual hesitance seemed to vanish—it was now replaced by a confidence and energy that Sayo had never seen before. She squinted, watching his profile illuminated by the light from the door.

kay. That's the end of today's lesson. See you tomorrow."

At the sound of the teacher's voice, all the students simultaneously pushed their chairs back and got noisily to their feet.

"Ugh, it's finally over."

"I'm starving."

"Do you have club today?"

The classroom was filled with a cacophony of voices. Sayo Yuzuki also stood up, neatly packing her textbook, notebook, and pencil into her bag. She glanced in the direction of the window and clocked the one empty seat amid all the ruckus.

"Absent again . . ."

It was, of course, the seat belonging to Rintaro Natsuki.

His not being there didn't make any difference to the atmosphere in the classroom; he wasn't one to cast much of a shadow. Nobody was particularly bothered by his absence. And until a few days ago, Sayo had been the same as everyone else.

But now things were different.

She could tell herself that it was because she was the class rep, or that she lived near him and needed to deliver his homework, but she knew that wasn't the real reason. The old image of Rintaro—that quiet boy with no presence and his nose perpetually in a book—floated into her mind. But now in the image he was accompanied by a ginger tabby cat.

"Hey, is Natsuki absent again?"

Sayo turned to see who had spoken. Just outside the door was a tall boy from the year above. Ryota Akiba, captain of the basketball team and brainiest student in the senior year, smiled at her. He was excessively cheery, attracting the ardent gaze of many of the female students.

"What do you want, Akiba?"

Sayo regarded him coldly.

Being on the student council together, the two were used to being in regular contact with each other, but today Sayo had no patience for his cockiness. She was never one for diplomacy when feelings were concerned; she was being pointedly unfriendly, but Akiba seemed amused.

"Seems Natsuki hasn't been coming to school. That's a problem."

"That doesn't sound very convincing coming from the senior who went AWOL along with him."

"Hey, I'm offended! All I did was pay a visit to a poor boy in need of some cheering up. He lost his grandpa, you know."

Akiba winked at a passing girl. His tactlessness made Sayo roll her eyes.

"Okay, well, if you're so into cheering him up, perhaps you'd like to pay that poor boy another visit and deliver his homework? I have yesterday's handouts here, too," said Sayo.

"What? You're not going to take them?" Akiba asked.

"I don't know how to cheer up a boy who's grieving over his grandpa. Maybe this is a situation best left to another boy."

"I hate to say it, but Natsuki and me—we have nothing in common—brains, athleticism, personality—nothing. We don't understand each other at all."

The smile didn't leave Akiba's face.

"That's just how it is," he concluded. "If you bought that book from his bookshop, then shouldn't you be the one to go?"

His eye was on the large volume that Sayo was holding.

"And by the way," he added, "I had no idea that the esteemed vice captain of the wind ensemble club was a connoisseur of vintage books."

"When I saw my classmate holed up in his bookshop reading, I thought I'd try reading something, too. But every time I open it up, my shoulders get horribly stiff. There's so many words. And so many pages!"

"Jane Austen was a good choice, though." Akiba's tone

changed slightly. "It's a great introduction to literature, and it's aimed at women. Good for Natsuki."

A soft light gleamed in Akiba's eyes.

Damn it, thought Sayo, sighing to herself. When book lovers talked about books, their faces seemed to light up.

A tad bewildered, she gripped her copy of *Pride and Prejudice* a little tighter.

"Okay, I'll leave the rest to you, Rin-chan."

The sound of the engine almost drowned out his aunt's perky voice, as her white Fiat 500 pulled away.

It was dusk and the sun was slipping away, the clear blue winter sky turning a deep shade of pink.

Rintaro watched the little car disappear into the distance, cheerfully waving so as not to cause her any concern. The moment he saw it turn the corner and disappear he let out a huge sigh.

"Please don't call me Rin-chan, Auntie . . ." he muttered.

His aunt's voice still rang in his ears.

"Rin-chan, you really need to get all your stuff packed and ready to move, okay?"

Since his grandfather died his aunt had been visiting him every day. Now she'd decided his moving day. Rintaro had grown to like his optimistic aunt more than he'd expected to. She was charmingly plump with a short stature, and as she crammed herself into her tiny white Fiat, she reminded Rintaro of a friendly dwarf in one of his old picture books. She was an extremely efficient worker, and the clearing of his grandfather's rooms was already well on its way.

"You know, if you live your life shut away in your room this way, it's like giving up completely," she'd told him—words that Rintaro knew were meant out of love. He knew she was right; he couldn't just hang around the bookshop forever, but he found himself frozen in inaction.

He'd just seen his aunt off when he spotted the class rep on the other side of the street. It felt as if he'd been rescued.

"What a rare sight: a hikikomori spotted in the outdoors."

She came over, her customary spring in her step.

"On your way home from school?"

"Not exactly. Absent again, weren't you? What the hell, Natsuki?"

Even though Sayo's gaze was cold, Rintaro found he didn't mind being on its receiving end. He quickly changed the subject.

"That was my aunt," he said, looking up the road. "She came to tell me to get ready for the move. The moving company's coming the day after tomorrow."

"Wow. That's soon!"

Sayo looked genuinely surprised.

"It's been almost a week since Grandpa died. I guess a poor little high school student like me can't be left alone forever."

"And yet you act just as if it's all happening to someone else. You're so calm about it."

"I'm not calm at all."

"Here you are again, stewing over things all alone as usual. If you don't stop thinking for a moment, your brain is going to overheat."

Sayo had pretty much nailed it. Rintaro grimaced.

"Well, at least this is the last time you'll have to deliver my homework to me."

"This isn't your homework, by the way."

Sayo held up the book she was carrying.

"I really enjoyed it."

It was Rintaro's turn to be surprised.

"You already finished it?"

"Yep. Thanks to you I ripped through it in two days. Barely slept."

She pretended to be annoyed, but there was a trace of a smile around her eyes. She looked toward the bookshop.

"Recommend me something else. If you're moving in two days, I'd better buy a few of them."

She went in without waiting for a reply. Rintaro hurried after her, but not two steps beyond the threshold he collided with her. Sayo had stopped in her tracks.

"What's up?" he asked, but he immediately saw what it was.

"Young love, Mr. Proprietor?"

Waiting inside was a certain large-size tabby cat with ginger fur and eyes of jade green. There was no trace of a smile on its face. It stood there in the central aisle under the bluish-white glow of the light that fell on the bookshelves.

"Good to see you've nothing important to do as usual," it continued.

"It so happens I'm busy getting ready to move."

"That's an obvious lie. Clearly you haven't even started yet."

Having dismissed Rintaro's objections, the tabby cat turned to Sayo and bowed its head with great gallantry.

"It's a pleasure to see you again. Thank you for taking such care of the proprietor here."

"You're very welcome," replied Sayo, obviously rather confused, but enjoying the situation nevertheless. This was the kind of adaptability that made her an excellent class rep.

"I didn't expect to see you again."

"Would you have preferred not to?"

"No, I was really happy to meet you. I had a wonderful time."

The cat shook its whiskers in delight at Sayo's earnest response, but then quickly turned its jade eyes on Rintaro.

"She's a rather open-minded and charming young woman. Such a contrast to the backward-looking, conservative youngster before me, who can't even act on his own feelings."

"I won't deny that, but it doesn't mean you're free to trespass in my shop. Every time you turn up without warning it doesn't exactly fill me with glee," Rintaro said.

"No worries," said the cat casually. "This'll be the last time."

"The last?"

"Right." The cat paused for a breath before continuing. "I need your help again."

"This is the final labyrinth," said the tabby cat, matter-of-factly.

Once again, Rintaro and Sayo found themselves walking along the inexplicably endless central aisle of Natsuki Books, its imposing stacks of books to either side of them, and lamps at intervals overhead.

"You've freed many books so far. Thank you for that."

"Unusual, coming from you."

Rintaro was a little taken aback by the cat's lack of venom.

"Is this all in preparation for you leaving us?"

"Partly."

As if to object to the cat's roundabout answers, Rintaro's tone became bolder.

"I was surprised when you turned up out of thin air. Are you going to surprise me again now by suddenly disappearing?"

"That's out of my paws. Cats are, by nature, creatures of will. They don't come and go at the convenience of human beings."

"At least the other cats I know don't have such a sharp tongue as you."

"Such a naive young boy! There are plenty of cats just like me."

The tabby didn't even bother to turn its head. Rintaro gave a pained smile.

"I'm going to miss your charming way with words."

"Don't get ahead of yourself. This is a conversation for after we've visited the next labyrinth."

The tabby suddenly stopped and looked back at Rintaro. There was a seriousness to its gaze that Rintaro hadn't seen before.

"The master of the third labyrinth is kind of a pain in the ass."

The cat turned its jade eyes on Sayo, who had been listening in silence.

"What?" she asked, frowning slightly.

"Our final adversary is a little different from the ones we've already met."

"Are you trying to tell us it's dangerous? Get us to turn back?"

The cat ignored the question and began to performatively wash its face.

"This adversary is extremely unpredictable. I'm sure that Mr. Proprietor here will be even more concerned for your safety."

"So now you're on Natsuki's side?" Sayo asked.

"Most certainly not," the cat retorted.

"No?"

"Your presence here blindsided me. But I can see now that it wasn't an accident."

Sayo and Rintaro looked at each other.

"You are likely here for a reason, so my hope is that you'll remain with us for our final journey."

"Hey—" Rintaro was starting to panic.

Ignoring him completely, the cat turned to Sayo and bowed its head.

"If anything happens to me," it said, in its deep and powerful voice, "please take care of Mr. Proprietor."

Sayo was silent for a moment, but then responded with her trademark charming smile.

"So you want my help?"

"Mr. Proprietor is reasonably intelligent. But because he lacks courage he tends to hesitate at the crucial moment. He's unreliable."

"I know what you mean."

"I'm aware that I'm dissing him right in front—"

Rintaro finally cut in.

"Look, Sayo, you don't have to go along with any of this."

"In the past I might not have, but now, Natsuki, I feel like if something happened to you, we'd both be in trouble."

Taken aback at Sayo's words, Rintaro clammed up. Sayo winked at him mischievously.

"Because then I wouldn't get that book recommendation I came here for."

The tabby cat chuckled.

"Splendid."

And with that, it spun back around and continued to walk ahead. Without hesitation, Sayo followed. Rintaro was left with no choice but to scurry to catch up to them. He was soon surrounded by a blinding white light.

The scenery on the far side of the light was different again. The first thing they saw was a long, gently meandering passageway. Sizewise it was the same as the one they had entered by, but in every other sense it was completely different. For one, there was a clear blue sky above. Unlike the dim, lamplit aisle of the bookshop, this was an outdoor structure. The walls were much taller than Rintaro, so he couldn't see beyond either side of them, but the bright sunlight overhead made the place feel open and airy. However, there was one thing that didn't mesh with the peaceful atmosphere.

It was Sayo who reacted first.

"Ah! What are all these?"

Her voice was shrill, almost a shriek. Although he didn't say anything, Rintaro was just as shocked.

The walls on both sides of the passageway were made of stacks of books—but there was nothing neat or orderly about the piles. Some books were torn, others crumpled, and the ones at the bottom were completely crushed by the weight of the upper books. There appeared to be no thought at all put into the stacking system, just tall piles of books reaching high into the sky. Even if you weren't a book lover like Rintaro, the sight would make anyone wince.

"Let's go!"

Everyone stopped gawping and got a hold of themselves. But there was nothing to say. The only way to express their current feelings was through silence.

Rintaro and Sayo nodded at each other and started to walk.

Making their way through the structure was like trying to find the exit for the most poorly designed modern art exhibit. Its passageway took erratic turns and without a clear view ahead, they soon lost all sense of direction. The decaying scenery was accentuated all the more by the bright sunlight.

They had no idea how far or for how long they had been walking when they came to a giant gray wall blocking the passageway. Sayo let out a sigh that sounded like relief.

"A dead end?"

"Is this it?" asked Rintaro, stopping and looking upward.

The giant wall before them was full of countless square windows and its top could not be seen, disappearing into the haze way overhead. Because of the walls of books on either side, it was hard to get the full picture, but the gray wall at the end of the passageway was possibly the side of a tall skyscraper.

They advanced a few steps farther to see that it was indeed a tall gray building, with a large glass doorway at its base. There was a sign above the door marked Entrance.

"I guess that means we should go in," said the cat, looking decidedly unimpressed. It headed straight for the door, which slid noiselessly open in welcome. A woman in a spotless, lavender-colored suit appeared out of nowhere and bowed to the three visitors.

"Welcome to World's Best Books, the world's number one publishing company."

She had a perfectly mechanical voice to match her perfectly mechanical smile. She also had a lot of nerve introducing her own company as the world's number one.

"May I ask your names and the reason for your visit?"

Caught off guard by the fake cheeriness of her voice, Rintaro struggled to speak.

"All those mounds of books outside the building, what are they?" he managed to ask.

"Outside the building?"

With that mechanical smile still anchored to her face, the woman tilted her head inquisitively about thirty degrees to the left. Rintaro couldn't help being a little impressed with her precision.

"Outside this building, there are books that are being horribly—"

"Oh my goodness, were you walking outside?" said the woman, putting her hand to her heart and frowning with concern. "I'm afraid that's terribly dangerous. I sincerely hope you weren't harmed in any way."

Rintaro began to feel incredibly weary, but the cat's calm voice was there to revitalize him.

"Stop this, Mr. Proprietor. This woman is not the one we've come to talk to."

"I suppose not," said Rintaro with a shrug.

The woman repeated her original question.

"May I ask your names and the reason for your visit?"

The question was delivered without affect but Rintaro took his time before replying.

"My name is Rintaro Natsuki. I'm here . . . to meet with the president of the company . . . I guess."

In response to Rintaro's awkward explanation, she bowed her head and went over to the reception desk. She made a brief phone call, then came back and bowed once more.

"Thank you for waiting. The president will see you now."

"Right now?"

"Of course. You've come all this way to visit him."

She delivered the information and immediately set off without waiting for Rintaro's response.

Rintaro couldn't tell if things were going well or badly. He had no idea what the president's purpose was, or even whether he had any purpose at all, but at least he was free of the pointless exchange.

"He must be a very open-minded president to agree to meet with visitors who turn up unannounced this way," remarked Rintaro.

"What on earth are you blabbering about?" said Sayo in his ear. "Company presidents are generally fat, balding men with a nasty personality. Watch out!"

Slightly disturbed by Sayo's prejudiced statement, Rintaro followed the woman along a long straight corridor. The floor beneath their feet was made of thick black granite, polished to such a sheen that they could see their own reflection. Along the center of this spotless gleaming floor ran a red carpet along which the woman now strode. After a while she stopped suddenly and turned to look at the three visitors.

"From this point you will be accompanied by a different guide."

Indeed, a little farther along the red carpet stood a man in a black suit. He gave an extremely low bow to Rintaro and the others.

"No bags or any other hand luggage is permitted beyond this point," he said, his voice monotone.

It went without saying that nobody was carrying any kind of hand luggage. The man simply recited his line, then without doing any kind of check, turned his back on the visitors and started walking. Rintaro and Sayo exchanged glances and set off after him.

After a short while they came across another man, this time wearing a blue suit. The color of his suit was the only thing that differentiated him from the previous guide. This man also gave an exaggerated bow.

"No authority or business titles permitted beyond this point," he said, without so much as a flicker of his eyebrow.

Having recited his line, just as the black-suited man had done before him, he turned his back and walked on.

"Is this some kind of joke?" Rintaro asked.

The tabby cat's response was not very encouraging:

"I don't think they're the joking type around here."

They followed the man in the blue suit, until they came across the next man, this time in yellow.

"No malice or hostility is permitted beyond this point," they were informed.

Rintaro was beginning to suspect the cat was correct.

They followed the yellow-suited man farther down the corridor, until suddenly they emerged into a large open hall. Rintaro and Sayo cried out in surprise. The space was wide and cylindrical in shape, so high that the ceiling was out of sight.

All around them, seemingly sprouting at random from the walls above, were hundreds of staircases, forming aerial walkways that crisscrossed and intertwined like a spider's web. It was like looking up at the detailed internal frame of some kind of spacecraft.

"Thank you for your patience," said the man in the yellow suit. He gestured toward the middle of the hall, where the red carpet ended at the doors of an elevator. At the elevator door stood a man in a red suit. As Rintaro and the others approached, he bowed deeply. The elevator doors opened to reveal a glass-walled interior.

"The president is waiting for you," he said tonelessly. "Please get in."

Just as the three were about to board the elevator, the man in the red suit moved to block the tabby cat's path. He gave another ceremonious bow.

"I'm sorry, but no dogs or cats are permitted beyond this point."

The tabby remained perfectly calm. As Rintaro opened his mouth to protest, the cat silenced him with a sharp look.

"I told you it'd be tricky this time," it said, turning to Sayo. "I'm glad you're here. I wouldn't be comfortable letting this one go on alone."

"I guess that must be why I'm here," said Sayo. She smiled, and the faint gleam of a grin seemed to pass through the cat's green eyes.

But then, as if to disperse any show of sentiment, the voice of the man in the red suit rang out with force.

"Kindly press the button for the top floor."

It turned out that there was in fact only one button in the elevator. There was a large panel with a single button, rather unnecessarily bearing the words *Top Floor*.

In other words, there was no button to come back down.

"It looks like we'll just have to get this sorted out, and then find our own way back," said Rintaro with a sigh. He turned his attention to the tabby cat on the outside of the elevator. There was a moment of silence.

"I'll be going then, partner."

"I'm counting on you, Mr. Proprietor."

Spurred on by the cat's confidence, Rintaro pressed the button. The doors sprang shut, and with a gentle shudder, the elevator began to move.

———

The elevator shot up into one of the aerial corridors, leaving the cat and the man in the red suit far below. It ascended with increasing speed through a three-dimensional geometric structure. There were intersecting lines all around. As far as the eye could see the stairways stretched around in every direction, but there was not a soul to be seen. Perhaps it was a trompe l'oeil painting.

"I'm glad they didn't make us climb all those stairs," muttered Rintaro. "What a pain that would have been."

Sayo smiled. She knew Rintaro was attempting to bring some levity to their surreal situation, even though he wasn't very good at it.

"It's incredibly unsettling."

"Yeah, even a foulmouthed, pointlessly pompous tabby cat is a better diversion than none at all."

Their eyes met and they both giggled.

Outside the elevator it was getting gradually darker. Although they were inside a building, it was as if the sun were slowly setting. The intricate structures began to fade into the darkness, and as their vision was getting poorer, it became impossible to tell whether the elevator was still climbing, or if it had come to a stop.

"At first I didn't even care if I could get home again," Rintaro said quietly.

Sayo didn't respond, but she turned to look at her friend.

"That first time the mysterious cat took me on a journey," he continued, "I thought that if it was a dream, I wouldn't mind never waking up and if it wasn't a dream then I wouldn't mind not being able ever to make it home again."

Rintaro adjusted his glasses.

"But ever since that cat turned up, I've been thinking more and more about everything that's been going on. I feel like I'm starting to see things a little differently."

"If this is what brings you out of your shell, it can only be a good thing," Sayo said.

Rintaro smiled wryly.

"I'm passive, I'll admit it, but I was really trying to keep you out of danger," he said.

"You know, Natsuki, sometimes you talk like you're trying out pickup lines. Is that a side effect of reading too many books?"

"Okay, let me rephrase. I'm sorry for getting you involved in this mess."

"You don't need to apologize. I'm having a great time here. And you know what? It's fun seeing a different side of you, Natsuki."

"Different how?"

"Forget I said anything," she said, laughing it off.

Sayo pictured Rintaro standing up to the white-coated scholar in that strange underground laboratory. It wasn't the first time she'd gone back to that image, but Rintaro would never know that.

Just as Rintaro was about to ask Sayo more questions, he felt the elevator slowing down to a stop. Once again, the door slid open noiselessly, revealing a dimly lit space beyond. It was almost impossible to make out the size or scale of the space because of how gloomy it was. However, a red carpet ran straight ahead, indicating where Rintaro and Sayo should go. At the far end was a heavy, wooden door with geometric patterns carved into it. There was something very intimidating about that door.

"Go on, Natsuki!"

"If you're asking me to . . ."

"You'll be fine."

Rintaro wasn't feeling brave, but he was encouraged by Sayo's steady voice.

"You've got more guts than you think, Natsuki. Especially when it comes to books. You've got nothing to be worried about at all. Even that kid Akiba is impressed by you."

Rintaro was thrown by her mention of him.

"Akiba?"

"Yeah. He was praising you at school the other day. He's a bit too cocky for my liking, but he's honest."

To Rintaro, these words were as refreshing as a clear winter sky. There was a warm feeling in the pit of his stomach that began to spread. It would be too much to call it courage, but it certainly came from the same place.

All of a sudden, he felt Sayo punch him gently in the back.

"Just make sure you bring me back, Natsuki."

They stepped gingerly out onto the carpet. It would be a lie to say he wasn't nervous, but Rintaro kept his gaze straight ahead. Something told him that now was the time to act. He took a deep breath and kept walking.

━━━━

"You really do love books, don't you?"

The voice of Ryota Akiba echoed in Rintaro's ears. Rintaro was only a junior, so he'd not really had much to do with this charismatic senior. It was his usual habit to stay away from any of the older students when they came by the bookshop. Akiba was the star player on the basketball team, the top academically in his year, and active on the student council. Rintaro, the hikikomori living shut up in his grandfather's bookshop, was from another world. Rintaro had once asked Akiba in all seriousness why a successful student like him would bother visiting the lowly Natsuki Books.

"Well, obviously because you have good books," he'd replied, clearly puzzled by Rintaro's question. "Your grandfather must be disappointed that you don't understand what a great place he has here."

And with that, Akiba had begun to sing the shop's praises.

"There are books here that are considered masterpieces all over the world. They've endured for years—until now. They're becoming more and more difficult to find in regular bookshops. But when I come here, I can find more or less anything I'm looking for."

He rapped his knuckles on the bookshelf before him.

"I get that bookshops might not carry something as eclectic as Andersen or Johnson, but these days even stuff written by Kafka or Camus is out of print. And it's practically impossible to find a shop that stocks the complete works of Shakespeare."

Akiba paused as if to consider why that was.

"Because they don't sell," he concluded. "Bookshops aren't volunteer organizations. They can't survive if they don't make sales, and that's why books that don't sell just disappear. That's why your grandpa's shop really stands out. There's an incredible assortment of books here on these shelves, even if they're no longer bestsellers—in fact, they take pride of place. I mean, of course it's because it's a used bookshop, but in here I can get my hands on anything but the absolute rarest of titles."

As he spoke he tapped on various bookshelves with his knuckles as if to emphasize his point.

"And on top of that," he added with a chuckle, "you have here an expert guide to all of these many difficult titles."

"A guide?"

"Do you have a copy of Constant's *Adolphe*? I saw something about it online the other day. It's supposed to be pretty good. I haven't been able to find it anywhere else."

Rintaro nodded and reached over to a bookshelf toward the back of the shop. He pulled out an old, worn book, the size of a medium-length novel.

"Benjamin Constant. His work is famous for its psychological depiction of human behavior—it's pretty unique. I think this one was written in France in the early nineteenth century."

Instead of reaching for it right away, Akiba paused to give the book and Rintaro a strange look, until he couldn't quite control his amusement any longer. He laughed in delight.

"You really do love books, don't you?"

That cheery laugh of his seemed out of place at Natsuki Books.

"Welcome to World's Best Books."

The booming voice greeted them as they ventured in through the tall, imposing door.

The room beyond the door was large, about the size of a high school classroom. From the ceiling hung a grand chandelier; below their feet, a plush carpet that completely muffled all sounds of their footsteps. And the walls on all four sides were covered with bright red curtains.

At the far end of this luxuriously decorated room was a desk with a glossy sheen, behind which sat a thin, elderly gentleman with an impressive head of white hair. He was dressed in a three-piece suit and leaned back at ease in his black office chair, his hands resting on the desk. He regarded his three visitors calmly.

"He's not what I expected," whispered Sayo. "It's weird for a company president not to be fat and balding. I bet he's just pretending to be the president. Maybe he's a midlevel manager working overtime."

Rintaro grinned. He found her tactlessness fascinating.

The man behind the desk raised his right hand.

"Please come in. I'm the company president," he said, gesturing toward a sofa. However, neither Rintaro nor Sayo felt like sitting. The sofa was extremely expensive-looking and covered with a thick layer of fur. The president didn't seem bothered by their refusal to sit.

"I really do appreciate your coming all this way to visit me. I know it must have been a difficult journey—I'm so far from the entrance, and security is extremely tight here."

"Our good friend wasn't allowed to come with us."

"Ah," said the president, narrowing his eyes. "I'm sorry about that. I'm afraid I hate cats."

"Oh . . . you're not a cat person?"

The kindly smile on the man's face suddenly faded and gave way to a sudden volley of words.

"No, not a cat person in the slightest. I detest them. Especially cunning ones."

117

The words flashed through the air like light reflecting off a knife blade.

The president may have sensed Rintaro stiffen, but he didn't show it.

"I do apologize for the trouble this may have caused to my guests from Natsuki Books."

"You know Natsuki Books?"

"Sure I do," he said, stroking his narrow chin. "No doubt it's a shabby old used bookshop, self-satisfied and stuck in the past. You must have piles of old-fashioned, difficult, unsellable books all over. Me, I'm envious. Sounds like running that store must be a walk in the park, free of any pressures or responsibilities."

The president flashed them a big grin.

It was a surprise attack—a declaration of war. Sayo winced, but Rintaro was undaunted. From the moment he'd set eyes on him, Rintaro knew there was something troubling this man. Perhaps the tabby cat was onto something.

The president continued on, completely unperturbed.

"I was fascinated to hear I had visitors from an antiquated old bookshop. It made me curious what kind of wild ravings they might share with me."

"You might want to rethink the decor of your office."

"Decor?" the president asked. When he'd said "wild ravings," he hadn't expected cutting remarks.

"Is this an office or a penthouse?" Rintaro continued. "These chandeliers are so glittery they'd give anyone a headache, and this carpet is so plush it's ridiculous. Such bad taste. Unless you're doing it for a joke, I'd suggest redecorating as soon as possible."

The president's eyebrows moved slightly, but his smile didn't falter.

Rintaro wasn't finished.

"I'm sorry if I sound rude, but my grandfather always taught me that it's a kindness to let someone know when their behavior's off, even if you antagonize them by doing so. And this room is so ugly I can't bear to look at it."

"Hey, Natsuki—"

Sayo hurriedly intervened. Rintaro finally stopped talking, wondering what he had just gotten himself into. This aggressiveness was out of character for him. He much preferred a careful, reasoned approach, even if that meant playing it safe. Above all, he valued moderate, constructive criticism. But the reason was clear to him. This time Natsuki Books—the shop itself—was being ridiculed.

The elderly president didn't move for a moment, and then finally let out a small sigh.

"Well, it seems I misjudged you. I had no idea there was a boy with such strong spirit at Natsuki Books."

"I don't know anything about spirit. I just love books."

"I see."

The president nodded generously, then seemed to think better of it. He shook his head instead.

"Love books?" he muttered to himself. "That's a problem."

He reached out a skinny arm toward a large button on his desk. He clicked it, and all at once the red curtains on three sides of the office began to open. Bright sunlight streamed into the room.

It took a while for Rintaro's eyes to adjust to the glare, so he didn't fully grasp the situation right off. Eventually he could see that they were in a room at the top of a skyscraper with windows on three sides. Beyond the windows there was a view of several other similar skyscrapers. Something white was pouring from the windows of the surrounding buildings and fluttering to the ground like snowflakes.

As Rintaro's eyes adjusted to the light, he heard Sayo give a small shriek. Then as he, too, realized what he was looking at, he gulped. The stuff that looked like snow—cascading from all the windows, hovering for a moment in the air, and then tumbling to the ground below—each and every piece was a book.

Someone was throwing books from the windows. They were caught by the wind and scattered far and wide. The buildings looked as if they were caught in a blizzard.

But it wasn't just the sky that was filled with books. When Rintaro and Sayo looked down from the window, the view was staggering. There on the ground were tens of, hundreds of thousands of books piled up—a veritable print wasteland.

As they looked on, stunned, they realized that some of the books were passing so close to the window that if they'd reached out, they could have touched them. That was when they realized that some of the books were being thrown from the same building they were standing in.

"Do you know what that is?" asked the president, with a smirk.

"Not exactly, but I know I don't like the sight of it," replied Rintaro.

"That's the new reality."

Rintaro's heart dropped.

"This building houses one of the largest publishing companies of our time. Every day we publish as many books as there are stars in the sky. For the people down there."

"But that's as if you're just spewing out wads of paper for no reason other than to increase the amount of waste."

"That's just how it goes," said the president nonchalantly. "We're a huge international publisher. Every day we produce mountains of books and sell them all over the world. With the profits we make from those sales, we fund the production of more books, which we then sell. We sell more and more, and our profits steadily increase."

The president fluttered his hand in a movement that mirrored the books passing the window. The gold rings adorning his fingers flashed in the sunlight.

Rintaro tried his best to comprehend the situation that the president was explaining, but it wasn't an easy task. Then he recalled the messy, disorganized piles of books they'd seen on their way. That bizarre landscape, and the sight of thousands of books falling through the sky before his eyes, coupled with the president's smooth voice—it all seemed to tie up his thoughts and drag him into a swamp of confusion. *Now he understood why the woman at the reception desk had been so concerned about the danger of walking outside*, he thought bitterly.

"You've got to be joking," he said. "Books aren't meant to be thrown. They're made to be read."

"You are so naive."

The president picked up a book at random from his desk.

"Books are expendable goods. It's my job to make sure they are consumed in the most efficient way possible. I couldn't do this job if I was some bookworm. Anyhow—"

He abruptly spun his black desk chair around, pushed open the window closest to him, and tossed the book he was holding straight out of the window. The book hung in the air for a moment as if there were something it had suddenly remembered, but then quickly disappeared out of view.

"This is what we do here."

Rintaro suddenly understood what the tabby cat had meant when it said this adversary would be different from the first two. The men he'd met in the other two labyrinths—no matter how bizarre their behavior—were, at heart, book lovers. By contrast, the man sitting in front of them right now didn't feel the slightest attachment to books. He treated them as trash and didn't feel even the teensiest bit bad about it. This was what the cat had meant when it said the man was extremely unpredictable.

"Natsuki, are you okay?"

It was Sayo's voice. Rintaro turned to look and met her intense gaze. He nodded and turned back to the man in the office chair.

"I came here today because a friend asked me to rescue some books."

"Rescue?"

"That's right. I think that means that I have to stop you."

"Well, that's a stupid thing to say. I've already told you that this is my job."

"But you're treating books as if they're nothing but scraps of paper. If that's the attitude of the people producing books, then nothing will reach the readers. The number of people who read books is already decreasing. If someone in your position has that kind of attitude, then the number of readers will just keep going down."

Rintaro put forth his best argument, but the president was unmoved. Beneath his white eyebrows, his eyes were unreadable, and the slight curve of a smile on his lips simply added to his elusive air.

After a moment, his narrow shoulders vibrated ever so slightly. Then the vibrations turned into a stronger shaking, and finally the president exploded with laughter. His low-pitched chuckling filled the room.

As Rintaro and Sayo stared, the president pressed his left hand to his mouth, as if to try to suppress his laughter. He rapped a couple of times on the desk with the knuckles of his right. Finally he began to speak.

"You really are an idiot, aren't you? Utterly dumb."

Even while he was cracking with laughter there was a bite to his words.

"No. In fact I don't think it's fair to call you an idiot. You're far from being the only one. These misconceptions are all too common these days."

"What misconceptions?" Rintaro asked.

"The one that books don't sell." The president laughed one more time, then continued. "You're deluded if you think books don't sell anymore these days. Books sell really well. In fact, World's Best Books is extremely successful."

"Is that supposed to be sarcasm?"

"It's not sarcasm at all. It's fact. It's very easy indeed to sell books—as long as you keep one fundamental rule in mind."

The president regarded Rintaro with amusement. It was clear he was enjoying himself. As if revealing the secret of an amazing magic trick, he lowered his voice to a whisper.

"Sell books that sell—that's the rule."

A curious phrase indeed. A curious phrase that had a bizarre ring to it.

"That's right," said the president. "Here at the world's number one publishing company, we don't publish books to inform or teach people. We print the books that society wants. We don't care about issues such as messages that need to be imparted, or philosophy that needs to be handed down to the next generation. We don't care about any harsh reality or difficult truths. Society isn't interested in things like that. Publishers don't need to worry about what they should be telling the world; they need to understand what the world wants to hear."

"It's dangerous to be that cynical."

"And you have an excellent mind to have noticed that it's cynical."

Chuckling, the president took a cigarette from a pack on his desk and calmly lit it.

"And yet, that's the reality. That's how we've managed to turn a steady profit."

Beyond the purplish curl of smoke, countless books went tumbling to the ground.

"If you were raised in that Natsuki Books fantasyland, then you should know this: In today's world, people don't have the time or the money to spend on 'literary masterpieces' or any fabulously long tome. But at the same time, reading is still fashionable. It confers status. Everyone wants to brag about reading some difficult book. And so, we publish our works with these people's needs in mind. In summary . . ."

He stuck his neck out to emphasize his point.

"Cheap digests and abridged versions sell like crazy."

He roared with laughter, his shoulders trembling.

"For those readers who desire a bit of stimulation, the best way is to do it with pornographic passages or gratuitous violence. And for those who lack imagination, adding a simple 'this really happened' does the trick. Your circulation is increased by several percentage points, and sales soar."

Rintaro felt sick to his stomach.

"And for those who never actually pick up a book, whether they can't get their hands on one, or can't be bothered to read, we produce information arranged by bullet point. Titles like *The Five Requirements for Success* or *The Eight Techniques to Get Ahead in Life.* People never catch on that they're being duped, that books like these are never going to help them get ahead. But the important thing is that my goal of selling books is accomplished."

"Stop it," Rintaro said.

"No. I'm not done yet."

There was no emotion whatsoever in the president's voice. The room temperature suddenly dropped by several degrees. A chill ran through Rintaro, although his forehead had broken out in sweat.

The president adjusted his chair and watched Rintaro from an angle.

"There's a big difference between the books you value and the ones that the rest of society wants," he said with pity in his eyes. "Think back—did you ever really have customers at Natsuki Books? Who even reads Proust or Romain Rolland nowadays? Would anyone cough up their hard-earned money to buy books like those? You know what most readers are looking for in a book? Something easy, cheap, and exciting. We have no choice but to adapt the form of books to suit those readers' tastes."

"That's really . . . Then, in that case . . ."

Rintaro searched desperately for the right words.

"Books just keep losing weight."

"Books losing weight? That's an interesting way of putting it. But poetic turns of phrase don't help with book sales."

"It's not all about sales. At least my grandpa believed in what he did and kept true to his beliefs till the end."

"So we should stock books that don't sell, so that World's Best Books can die along with all the world's greatest works of literature? Just like Natsuki Books did?"

Rintaro glared back at the president. Glaring was all he could do.

"Nobody's interested in truth or ethics or philosophy. People are worn out from living. All they want is either to be stimulated or healed. The only way for books to survive in such a world is for them to metamorphose. Dare I say it? Sales *are* everything. No matter how great a masterpiece, if a work doesn't sell it vanishes."

Rintaro felt slightly dizzy and put his hand to his forehead. He touched the rim of his glasses, but as usual, no coherent thought came to him. The words he was hearing were too far beyond anything he could have imagined. He knew he could talk to his heart's content about the value and appeal of books. But to this man before him, books had a completely different value—one that Rintaro had never considered. This man lived in a whole other world.

"It's okay, Natsuki."

It was Sayo's voice. He felt her strong presence by his side. Sayo had stepped up and had taken a firm grip of his left arm.

"You're okay."

"I don't feel okay, though."

"But you are."

She glared at the man behind the desk.

"Everything he's saying is wrong. I'm certain of it."

"Yeah, but his logic makes sense."

"This isn't about logic," she said decisively. "I don't know anything about that. What I can say is that he sounds like he doesn't even believe half the things he's telling you."

Rintaro turned his head to look at Sayo. And in that moment, he recalled the tabby cat's words: "This labyrinth runs on the power of truth . . . But not *everything* he says is true . . . There's got to be a lie in there somewhere."

Yes, that's right, thought Rintaro. He had been overwhelmed by how extreme the man's words had been. But something about them didn't quite add up.

Once again, Rintaro reached up and touched his glasses frame.

"Thinking won't help you, Rintaro Natsuki," said the president serenely, his words accompanied by a thick cloud of cigarette smoke. "You're still young. There are realities of life that you don't want to accept. I, on the other hand, am intimately familiar with how the world works. Your feelings about a book don't determine its value. The number of copies in circulation does. In other words, in our society it is the banknote that is the arbiter of value. Those who forget this rule and try to embrace something idealistic have no choice but to drop out of society altogether. It truly is a shame."

The president spoke like a preacher—his speeches resembled sermons. It was a blatant attempt to gaslight Rintaro, to throw his chain of thought out of whack. However, Sayo's grip on his arm was firm, as if to offer support.

As the president quietly chuckled to himself, Rintaro thought furiously.

He thought and thought, and then finally stepped forward. The president's laughter and his thick cigarette smoke had formed a kind of fog in the air, but Rintaro seemed to cut his way through the fog. He didn't falter.

"It's true that Natsuki Books isn't your average second-hand bookshop."

Rintaro looked at his formidable adversary behind his grand desk.

"We don't have many customers and we don't sell that many books. But it's a very special place."

"Yes, there's a word for that—despair," said the president, shaking his head. "And it's the perfect word for my current state of mind. Really, your personal sentiments are of no concern to me."

"But it's not personal. Every single customer who came in the door felt the same way I do. That little used bookshop was filled with my grandfather's thoughts and feelings—anyone who stepped over the threshold could feel them. And that's what made it special."

"Well, that's vague. Nobody's going to be convinced by an abstract argument like that. Would you mind being a bit more specific about your grandfather's *thoughts* and *feelings*?"

"I don't need to explain it to you. I know—because I'm just like you."

Rintaro's words, delivered very quietly, had the power to stop the president in his tracks. He didn't move again for a while. The plume of smoke that rose from between his fingers gradually thinned then finally petered out.

Eventually he narrowed his eyes slightly and opened his mouth.

"I don't know what you mean by that."

"That's another lie."

The president's eyebrows twitched.

"You said just now that books are expendable goods. You claimed your job is impossible to do if you love books."

"That's correct."

"That's a lie."

Rintaro's voice was blunt.

A line of ash fell from the president's cigarette.

"You said it just now: books need to metamorphose if they are to survive. If you really just saw books as expendable goods, you would never have said that."

"Humph. That's a questionable line of reasoning."

"It's all about the nuances. If you really think of books as nothing but scraps of paper, then you ought to quit this job. But I hear from you that you are committed to changing the form of books so they will survive. That means you like books. That's why you're still sitting there. Just like my grandpa . . ."

Rintaro's voice trailed off into a heavy silence. The room remained silent apart from the occasional swish of a book falling past the window. But there were fewer than before.

The president regarded Rintaro awhile, then spun his chair around to observe the bleak landscape beyond the windows.

"It doesn't matter anymore. It doesn't matter what I

think—we have to face reality. Books are getting thinner and thinner, and people are flocking to them. And then books need to respond to the demands of the flocks. No one can stop the cycle. And isn't Natsuki Books proof of this? No matter how special or welcoming the atmosphere, the number of customers won't go up. Am I wrong?"

"Not true!"

Sayo's voice made its way through the stuffy air of the room like a fresh breeze.

"Natsuki Books's customer base isn't dying. For example we have Akiba . . . he doesn't have the greatest personality, but he is extremely smart. And there's me. I've also become a regular."

It wasn't exactly something to shout from the rooftops, but Sayo stood there with unwavering pride.

"Fine," said the president, "but that amount of business just isn't profitable. If you're not selling, then it's meaningless. Bookshops aren't charities."

"Well then," Rintaro cut in, "exactly how much profit do you need to make?"

"How much?"

The president's eyes widened at the unexpected question.

"My grandpa used to say once you got thinking about money there was no end to it. If you have one million yen, then you want two. If you have one hundred million, then you want two hundred. So better to stop focusing on money and talk instead about the book we read today. Like you, I believe that bookshops need to turn a profit. But I do know that there are things just as important as making money."

Rintaro was no longer trying to persuade or win an argument. He was simply speaking from the heart.

"If you're a producer of books, you should never call them 'expendable goods,' no matter how much things don't go as you'd hoped. You should shout 'I love books' from the rooftops—don't you agree?"

The president screwed up his eyes as if dazzled by the light.

"Even if I were to say that, would it make any difference?"

"Of course it would," replied Rintaro, quick as a flash.

"But if I admit I love books, how will I be able to publish ones that I don't like?"

The president's eyes widened slightly and the corners of his mouth twitched.

It took a moment for Rintaro and Sayo to realize he was smiling. They also noticed that at some point the books had stopped falling. Everything was quiet. Time stood still.

"With that approach, you're going to have a hard life ahead of you," said the president finally, looking Rintaro straight in the eyes.

Rintaro didn't look away.

"Sitting behind that desk calling books expendable goods— I would call that a hard life."

"Would you, now?"

As the president murmured those words, the door to the room opened and the woman from the reception desk entered.

"It's about time—" she said, but the president raised a hand to cut her off. She stepped back out again.

The president paused for a moment, then indicated the door through which she'd just exited. It slid open, this time to reveal the red carpet that led back to the elevator.

Not a word was exchanged. Rintaro looked at Sayo, and the two turned to leave. They'd barely taken a few steps when the president finally spoke.

"I wish you the very best of luck."

Rintaro turned back to look at the man behind the desk. It was difficult to read any emotion in the light of his eyes. He waited a beat.

"You, too."

The president was probably not expecting this response. His eyes widened, and this time, the corners of his mouth clearly curved upward. Rintaro caught a glimpse of a most unexpected grin.

———

"Thanks."

The tabby cat, padding noiselessly through the rows of books, looked back over its shoulder at Rintaro and Sayo.

"Looks like you did good."

"I don't know about that, but the president did smile as he sent us on our way," Rintaro said.

"That's good enough." The cat nodded.

The bluish light, countless books filling the space on both

sides, and the lamps hanging overhead. This bizarre scene had become a familiar one to them. They were on their way home, led through the strange corridor of books by the tabby cat.

After the brief words of thanks, the cat continued in silence. The very fact that it wasn't talking spoke volumes.

"So you said this last labyrinth would be the end . . ." ventured Rintaro.

"That's right," said the cat as it came to a halt. They were back in Natsuki Books. Almost as if the whole long trip had been an illusion, the way back had been simple and short.

After walking them to the heart of the shop, the cat turned nimbly around and headed back up the aisle.

It hadn't bothered to say goodbye.

"Are you going?" Rintaro spoke up.

"Yes, I'm afraid I have to."

The cat turned and bowed deeply.

"Thanks to you, many, many books have been freed. I'm truly grateful."

The cat remained in that humble pose, its head lowered, backlit by the bluish-white glow. It was a strange sight, but the emotion the cat expressed was sincere.

"You have vanquished the inhabitants of three labyrinths with your own power. My work here is done."

Sayo jumped in.

"What do you mean, 'done'? Won't we see you again?"

"No, we can't meet. There's no longer a need."

"But . . ." Sayo began, turning to Rintaro in bewilderment.

Rintaro let out a deep sigh.

"If this really is goodbye, then there's something I want to say first," he said.

"Go ahead," replied the cat. "Say whatever you want. A complaint, a parting shot at me—whatever."

"I just want to say thank you. That's all."

Rintaro bowed.

Both Sayo and the tabby cat seemed surprised.

"Hold on, was that sarcasm?"

"Of course not," said Rintaro, a wry grin on his face. "I'm not as dumb as you think, you know."

"Not as dumb as I think . . . ?" said the cat, looking at Rintaro suspiciously.

"You came to me saying you needed to free some books and that you needed my help. But I think your goal was really something else."

The cat didn't stir, just fixed Rintaro with its jade eyes.

"The day I lost my grandfather I couldn't care less what happened to me. My mom and dad were gone, and now I'd lost Grandpa, too. It was all so unfair and I was just so sick and tired of everything, and then suddenly you turned up."

He scratched his head a little shyly.

"If you hadn't, I definitely wouldn't be standing here with a smile on my face. I was supposed to help you, but you're the one who helped me."

Rintaro looked at the cat and took a deep breath before continuing.

"I shut myself away in the shop, but you forced me out of it. Thank you."

"Shutting yourself away in a bookshop is fine," said the cat in its rich, deep voice. "What worried us more was that you'd retreated into your own shell."

"My shell . . ."

"Please do come out of it."

The cat spoke quietly, but its voice resonated to the pit of Rintaro's stomach.

"Don't give in to loneliness. You aren't alone. You have many friends looking out for you."

Its parting words were heartfelt, encouraging. Rintaro fought off the questions that came to his head and simply looked back in silence.

Only a few days had gone by since his grandfather had passed away, and yet thanks to this strange cat, somehow he had been able to find some light in the darkness of his misery. That had been the cat's true gift.

"Thank you," Rintaro repeated.

"Good manners," said the cat with a chuckle.

The cat flashed him one last smile, bowed gracefully, then slipped away down the bookshop aisle. As it was enveloped in the light, it began to scamper away at full speed. Sayo and Rintaro watched it disappear without glancing back.

The figure of the cat dissolved into the soft blue light and was replaced by the old wooden back wall of the bookshop.

Although there wasn't a single customer in sight, the doorbell rang once, bright and clear.

THE FINAL LABYRINTH

intaro tipped the white teapot and immediately the aroma of Assam tea rose from the well-used Wedgwood teacup. He added a single sugar cube and plenty of milk, then took a silver spoon and gently stirred, watching the splash of milk gently circle the cup and become absorbed into the tea. He nodded with satisfaction.

"I've gotten really good at this."

Brewing tea, that is.

It had been his grandfather's habit to make himself a cup of tea after cleaning the bookshop every morning. Rintaro had followed the same routine for the past week and was beginning to feel very comfortable in it.

"Rin-chan!"

The high-pitched voice came from the direction of the door. Rintaro looked up to see the round, friendly face of his aunt.

"It's moving day! Are you ready?"

She's still calling me Rin-chan, he thought. With a smile he put down his cup and headed for the door.

Dressed in a white apron, Rintaro's aunt seemed more approachable than ever; she must've been over fifty, but her air and mannerisms were those of a younger woman.

Outside the sky was cloudy, but somehow the air was bright, not only in contrast to the dimly lit shop, but also because Rintaro's aunt always managed to bring a sunny disposition with her that warmed any chill.

"Will the moving truck be arriving this afternoon, Aunt?"

"Ugh, stop that, Rin-chan," she replied. "When you speak formally like that, my shoulders go all stiff."

Rintaro saw his aunt's Fiat 500 parked outside. The image of her stuffed into that tiny car made him smile.

"I'm going shopping. Wondered if you wanted anything?"

They walked out together. Easing herself back into the car, she added, "I'll be back by midday. Don't worry, I'll bring you some lunch. Make sure you're ready!"

Rintaro smiled and nodded at this rapid succession of statements. But as she got ready to drive away, she suddenly stopped and looked up at him.

"There's something different about you, Rin-chan. You know, I was really worried about you when I saw you at the funeral. It looked as if you were just going to fade away. But it turns out you're stronger than I thought."

"I'm holding up," said Rintaro, with the most cheerful expression he could muster. "Not perfectly of course, but I'm about as fine as I could be."

His aunt smiled, then suddenly looked up at the sky and exclaimed, "Oh!" Rintaro followed her gaze and opened his eyes slightly.

"It's snowing," she said.

Fluffy white snowflakes fluttered down around them. There was no sunshine, but the glittering flakes made everything seem bright. Passersby stopped to look up at the sky.

"I love it when it snows. It's so exciting."

Rintaro's aunt always spoke spontaneously like this. She turned to Rintaro, her voice high and girlish.

"I'll buy you a cake tonight, Rin-chan."

"A cake? Why?"

"Well, it's Christmas Eve, isn't it?"

Rintaro was genuinely surprised. Ever since his grandfather had passed away, he had lost track of the calendar. He looked around at the street and realized that the trees and the eaves of houses were decked out in colored lights. It was as if all the people and the houses they lived in were excitedly preparing for Christmas, while Rintaro and Natsuki Books alone were opting out.

"Or were you planning to spend the evening with that lovely girlfriend of yours?"

"I don't have a girlfriend."

"I'm just teasing."

Rintaro's aunt revved up the engine.

"See you later!" With one more cheerful laugh, she drove away.

Rintaro looked up and down the street. Delivery bikes were passing groups of high school students on their way to morning club activities. He didn't associate any particular feelings or memories with Christmas Eve, but he did feel emotional as he realized that this would be the last time to enjoy this particular scenery. Even the falling snow seemed to be meaningful. He stood for a while and took it all in.

Only ten days had passed since his grandfather's death—a short period of time, and yet it felt long to Rintaro because of all the strange events that had happened to him since. And of all those events, the thing that had stuck in his mind was the way the tabby cat had smiled at him right before it left for good.

It was three days ago that he'd last seen those fluffy tiger stripes. Since then the days had flown by as he prepared for the move. The cat had not shown up again, and the back wall of the bookshop had remained just as it always was.

Sayo had dropped by each day, both on her way to and from school, to drink a cup of tea with Rintaro, and to discuss the Stendhal novel she was currently reading. But he reckoned she was probably more curious about the cat's whereabouts. And of course, Rintaro himself would be lying if he said he wasn't curious himself.

But time is merciless in its passing.

This was something that Rintaro understood all too well. No matter how sad, how painful, how nonsensical a thing might happen, time refused to stand still and wait for him. Somehow he had just drifted along until here he was today.

Eventually Rintaro composed himself and headed back into the bookshop. He started to put away the tea things, but then suddenly stopped in his tracks.

The back of the bookshop was bathed once again in the bluish light. And right there, with its back to the light, sat a large tabby cat.

"It's been a while, Mr. Proprietor."

Rintaro's shock eventually gave way to a wry smile.

"It's only been three days."

"Really? Has it?"

"Am I supposed to welcome you back?"

"No need to stand on ceremony."

The cat turned its jade eyes from the bluish light.

"I need your help."

Behind the cat, the light began to intensify, revealing row upon row of books.

"Just one last time."

As always, the cat's speech and actions were abrupt, with no greetings or explanations. There was no hint of celebration at their reunion.

"I thought we were saying goodbye."

"Things have changed. We have to enter a labyrinth again."

The cat's tone of voice was as nonchalant as ever, but there was a tension behind it that hadn't been there before.

"What's going on?"

"A fourth labyrinth has materialized."

"A fourth one?"

"Yes, this was an unforeseen situation. I'm going to need your help again. But . . ."

Its tone changed.

"Our next adversary is on another level. It's a whole new ball game."

The cat's voice was blunt and imperious as ever, but it lacked that usual edge. It was a sign that something was amiss.

"If they're that tough, are you sure you want me to help?"

"It has to be you. They've asked for you specially."

"The opponent has?"

"It's a tricky one. This time there's a real possibility of never coming back. But you'll work it out somehow."

The cat almost sounded as if it were pleading with him.

"Got it," said Rintaro simply. "Let's go."

His reply took the cat by surprise. It took a while to respond. Its green eyes observed the boy keenly.

"You heard me, right? I said it was dangerous."

"I also heard you say that it would be different from everything till now . . . we might not be able to get home."

"And you're still prepared to come?"

"You're in trouble. That's enough for me," Rintaro said.

The tabby cat looked as if it had just seen a ghost in broad daylight.

"Are you feeling well, Mr. Proprietor?"

"I'll go."

"But . . ."

"I wanted to thank you. I mean I did tell you as much, but I haven't actually done anything to repay your kindness. This is the perfect chance."

There was a brief pause as the tabby cat stared at Rintaro awhile, then it nodded with more emotion than it'd ever shown before.

"I appreciate the help."

"Just . . ." added Rintaro. "I want to set out immediately."

He hurried over to the front door of the shop, closing and locking it right away.

"It's about the time Sayo comes over. If she hears us talking, she'll want to come with us. I don't want to get her involved." Rintaro smiled. "Especially if it's going to be more dangerous."

The cat accepted his concern in silence, before gazing at Rintaro with an unusually stern expression.

"Unfortunately, she's already involved."

In the awkward silence that followed, Rintaro stopped what he was doing and raised an eyebrow. A passing cyclist rang their bell as they passed in front of the shop. The cat began to speak.

"Sayo Yuzuki has been taken. She's locked up in the deepest part of the labyrinth."

Rintaro froze.

"Did you hear me, Mr. Proprietor?"

"I don't understand . . ."

"What's not to understand? Sayo has been kidnapped. Our last quest goes beyond saving books."

The cat looked sharply at Rintaro.

"We're on a mission to rescue your friend."

Rintaro shifted his eyes toward the passageway that led out of the back of the shop. A long, straight aisle, packed with books, illuminated by that eerie blue glow.

"Why?"

From within Rintaro emerged a sickening dread.

———

"You're not coming to school after all, are you?"

Two days previously, early in the morning, Sayo had said those words to him. She'd popped in as usual on her way to band practice. She was irritated to find Rintaro once again skipping school, sitting at the cash desk with his cup of morning tea.

They'd chatted awhile, but Rintaro couldn't remember what about. Just chitchat, probably. About books, about tea, and a little about the cat. Afterward, just as she was leaving for her practice, she'd turned around.

"You can't stay shut away here forever. I know there's plenty of stuff that's not worth the effort, but this is your life—"

Sayo broke off and then continued in a softer voice.

"You need to hold your head high and step out on your own."

It was the typical advice of a class rep, but he also knew it was Sayo's way of comforting him about the move.

Rintaro had appreciated her encouragement.

He narrowed his eyes. Burned into his retina was the sight of her hand waving goodbye to him that very morning.

"It's strange," he said, as he followed the cat down the long aisle of books. "I've never been so worried about another person in my life."

The cat threw him a glance but didn't say anything.

The corridor seemed longer than the last time. It was hard to tell whether it was just Rintaro's imagination or something else entirely.

"Why did they take Sayo? If they wanted me, why didn't they just take me in the first place?"

"No idea," replied the cat, bitterly. "You'll have to ask them yourself. I guess they thought the key to getting through to you was the girl."

"What are you talking about?"

"It's obvious, isn't it? That girl cares about you," the cat said, staring straight ahead. "She's always worrying about her gloomy classmate . . ."

"That's because Sayo's responsible. She has to be, she's the class rep. And she's a good neighbor—"

"I don't know if this will be of any help to you," the cat interrupted, "but I can tell you one thing. When that girl first came to the bookshop, I told you that only certain people were able to see me, and under special conditions. I wasn't talking about supernatural powers or anything like that."

This time the cat stopped and turned to face Rintaro.

"All it takes is compassion."

"Compassion?" Rintaro said, dumbfounded.

"Being able to express shallow words of sympathy in a sweet voice doesn't make someone a caring, compassionate soul. What's important is the ability to have empathy for another human being—to be able to feel their pain, to walk alongside them in their suffering."

The tabby cat resumed walking and Rintaro scrambled as usual to keep up with its pace.

"That's not a special or unusual power," the cat continued. "It's a natural ability that everyone possesses. The problem is that most people have lost touch with that ability in the hustle and bustle of their daily lives. Like you have."

Rintaro was speechless.

"In our stifling daily lives, we're all so occupied with ourselves that we stop thinking about others. When a person loses their own heart, they can't feel another's pain. They lie, they hurt others, use weaker people as stepping-stones to get ahead—they stop feeling anything. The world has become full of those kinds of people."

As if in reaction to the cat's shift in tone, the corridor began to change. The simple wooden bookcases that lined its walls gradually turned into heavy, inlaid oak shelves and the corridor itself began to expand—the ceiling rising and the walls receding until it was wide enough for five or six people to walk side by side. The overhead lamps disappeared and the place was lit instead by a row of candles set out at intervals on the floor. Along its center, one human boy and one cat walked for a while in silence.

"And yet in a world so apparently beyond redemption, sometimes someone like Sayo comes along. It's impossible to fool someone with a heart like hers. That girl wasn't helping you out of some kind of duty. She was genuinely concerned for your well-being."

The flames of the candles swayed slightly, although there wasn't a single breath of wind.

Now that the cat had put it into words, Rintaro realized it was true. He thought of all the times Sayo had come back to Natsuki Books. All of a sudden each scene took on a greater significance in his mind.

"If you're worrying about her now, that means you're finding your own heart again. You're not just thinking about yourself, but you're feeling compassion for others."

"Compassion for others . . ."

"That friend of yours is a little too good for a wimp like you," the cat said with a hint of amusement.

Rintaro looked up. Far above was a gently curving vaulted ceiling with the beauty and serenity of a classic old church dome.

"There's so much that I think I understand but actually don't," Rintaro said.

"The fact that you're already aware of that is the first step."

"I do feel a little braver."

"A little won't be enough." The cat lowered its voice. "The final opponent is truly formidable."

Barely had it finished speaking when a gigantic wooden double door appeared before them. It looked too heavy for Rintaro's feeble arms to handle, but as they approached, it began to creak its way open.

Both sides slowly opened to reveal an expanse of lush green grass beyond. Leafy trees stretched up into the sky and white fountains dotted the landscape. Each fountain was adorned with statues, and the neatly trimmed hedges contrasted beautifully with the geometric paving stones laid out beneath.

Rintaro and the cat were standing on a wide patio with a porch roof over their heads, looking out over all this. On each side of them a stone-paved path sloped gently away into the garden. It felt as if they had stumbled into the grounds of a massive Western-style medieval mansion.

"Quite the elaborate design," the cat murmured, just as a rattling sound came from their right. They looked over and saw a carriage drawn by two horses approaching along the pathway.

The carriage stopped before them, and the elderly coachman climbed down from the driver's seat. Wordlessly, he bowed to the two of them and opened the carriage door.

"I suppose you want us to get in," said the cat, jumping right in without waiting for an answer. The elderly driver remained with his head bowed until Rintaro followed suit.

The interior was surprisingly spacious and upholstered in red velvet. Rintaro and the cat seated themselves facing each other.

The door shut with a clack, and after a moment's pause, it began to move.

"What's all this about?" said Rintaro.

"I think it's all to welcome you."

"I'm afraid I don't know of anyone who would want to welcome me quite this way."

"Even if you don't know them, they certainly know you. You're quite the celebrity in this world."

"This world?"

"And its ruler is a very special being. They possess incredible powers."

"Wow, so I ought to be moved to tears that I've been invited here? Should I thank them for kidnapping my friend or something?"

The cat gave a small laugh.

"That's a good approach. Logic and reason are never the best weapons in an irrational world."

"Humor is, right?"

As Rintaro spoke, the carriage lurched and picked up speed. They were on a major road now. He looked out of the window to see the vast garden rolling past. Sunshine, breeze, splashing fountains—everything was pleasant, but at the same time there was something uncanny. Rintaro could detect no signs of life, and by that he didn't mean human life only. There were no birds, no butterflies, no sign of anything that sustained this world. In other words, it didn't matter how beautifully it was dressed up, this place was not real.

"This will be the last time I ever speak to you," said the cat.

Rintaro turned his gaze from the scenery outside to look at his companion.

"That's not the first time I've heard that from you."

"Try to focus on yourself."

Perched on the old-fashioned carriage seat, the cat turned its jade green eyes to stare straight into Rintaro's.

"This time really will be the last."

"Well, I have a bunch of questions for you before you go."

The cat stared at him. Rintaro paused a moment, then laughed awkwardly.

"The thing is, I have no idea where to start."

The light that fell on its face gradually turned the cat's fur a deep crimson. Outside the carriage, daylight was quickly fading from dusk to night, and the interior began to sink into gloom. Rintaro looked up and saw that stars had already begun to twinkle in the night sky.

Suddenly the cat spoke.

"Books have a soul."

Its beautiful eyes seemed to capture the light of the stars and they, too, twinkled in the darkness.

"A book that sits on a shelf is nothing but a bundle of paper. Unless it is opened, a book possessing great power or an epic story is mere scraps of paper. But a book that has been cherished and loved, filled with human thoughts, has been endowed with a soul."

"A soul?"

"That's right," replied the cat emphatically. "These days people rarely pick up books anymore, nor do they infuse them

150

with their thoughts. Books are gradually losing their souls. But there are still a few people like you and your grandfather who love books with every fiber of their being. You really listen to their message."

The cat slowly turned its head and looked up at the starry sky.

"You are a truly valuable friend to us all," it added.

It was a curious thing to say, but each word sank deeply into Rintaro's heart.

The cat's eyes gleamed. Noble, confident to the point of arrogance, and yet beautiful. An amazing cat.

"You know, I feel as if I've known you for a long time," said Rintaro suddenly.

The cat didn't turn its head, but its pointed ears twitched as if to encourage the boy to continue.

"A really long time. Back when I was a little boy . . ."

Rintaro looked up at the carriage roof as if searching his memory.

"I met you once in a story. I think it was one my mother read to me."

"Books have souls," repeated the cat softly. "A cherished book will always have a soul. It will come to its reader's aid in times of crisis."

The calm, measured voice warmed Rintaro's heart. He looked over and saw the cat faintly smiling.

"I told you that you weren't alone."

The carriage carrying the two friends raced on through the night. Through the windows, starlight fell on its velvet interior. Spotlighted by the pale light, the cat's smile abruptly faded and its eyes flashed.

"However, a book with a soul is not always an ally."

Rintaro frowned.

"Is this about Sayo?"

"I'm talking about this final labyrinth."

The cat turned back to the window. Rintaro followed its gaze. The stars in the sky shone lustrous and beautiful, but they seemed to be arranged completely at random. He couldn't make out a single familiar constellation.

"Just as a person's soul can be warped by suffering, so can the soul of a book. A book that has been in the hands of a person with a twisted soul will also acquire a twisted soul. And together they run amok."

"A book's soul can be warped?"

The cat nodded emphatically.

"Older books, particularly those that have a long history, have been influenced by the minds and souls of a great many people. Those books become imbued with a tremendous power, whether it be good or evil. And when the soul of such a book becomes distorted . . ."

The cat sighed.

"Well, it ends up wielding a power far greater than I or any other could ever hope to have."

"I think I'm starting to understand what you meant when you said this adversary is different from all the others."

Rintaro's tone was unusually calm and collected. In fact, he felt far more relaxed than he had ever been.

Outside, the scenery had somehow changed again. The vast landscaped garden was now an old town. The buildings were mostly two-story, bicycles leaning up against their walls; yellow streetlights flickered, and here and there old-fashioned vending machines gave off a whitish glow. It was a scene that Rintaro had seen somewhere before.

"I'm sorry, Mr. Proprietor." The cat bowed. "What lies ahead is out of our control."

"No apology necessary," replied Rintaro with a grim smile. "I really appreciate everything you've done for me."

"I haven't done anything," said the cat. "You have come this far under your own steam."

"But still—" began Rintaro, as the carriage's shaking ceased, and it seemed to be slowing down. "I've learned a lot, thanks to you. I know what's important now."

And with that, the carriage shuddered to a stop. After a brief pause, the door opened. A chill wind blew in, making Rintaro's spine tingle.

Looking out, he saw a familiar landscape. He took his time climbing out, past the overly courteous driver. When he turned back to look for the cat, he saw that it hadn't stirred and remained in the darkness of the carriage's interior, watching him with those jade eyes.

"Aren't you coming?"

"No need. You're ready to go on your own now."

The cat gave him a glowing smile.

"Go ahead, Rintaro Natsuki."

"That's the first time you've called me by my name."

"You've earned my acknowledgment. The twisted soul is strong—"

The cat paused.

"But you are stronger."

Powerful words of encouragement, which could only have been uttered by a true friend.

As Rintaro nodded, he felt an unpleasantly cold sensation trickle down his back. But he didn't want to run away. He couldn't run away.

"Will I see you again?"

"Quit it, will you? That's way too cliché for a farewell speech."

The cat was back to his old self. Almost.

"Farewell, my brave friend."

The perfect parting words.

The cat bowed its head respectfully to Rintaro, who returned the gesture. The boy turned his back to the carriage and began to walk. Ahead of him, at the end of a narrow street, was a single yellow streetlight. Huddled beneath it was a little old house. Rintaro strained to make out the wooden sign hanging over the wooden latticed door. It read NATSUKI BOOKS. It was a perfectly detailed re-creation.

Undaunted, Rintaro marched straight ahead. No matter how cleverly done, a fake was still a fake. There was no moon in the night sky, and below it no trees or grass. There were no lights on in the neighboring houses. Never had he seen a more comfortless scene.

Rintaro cut straight through the chill of the night, up to

the stone steps in front of the bookshop. Beyond the familiar latticed door shone the only clear light in the whole scene.

A voice rang out.

"Come in!"

It was a woman's voice, perfectly calm. At the same moment, the door began to open.

———

"Welcome, young Rintaro Natsuki."

The voice was flat. Rintaro looked around. He was in Natsuki Books but it looked very different from usual. There was not a single book on the shelves that lined the walls, making the place feel empty and cavernous. In the center of the room were a pair of matching sofas, facing each other—something that had never been there before. Seated on the sofa facing the door was a slight figure. Rintaro was surprised to make out a thin, elderly woman dressed in a formal black dress. She was sitting on the large sofa with her legs crossed and her long, white hands resting on her knees. She stared at Rintaro in a way that made her seem utterly helpless and defenseless, but at the same time there was a strangely gray aura about her that made her look unapproachable.

"What happened to your cat attendant?"

Besides her lips, not a muscle in her whole body moved.

"It told me to go on alone."

"How cold. What an unfeeling friend you've got."

She brushed her long fingers across her cheek.

"Someone as powerful as I am deserves a little more respect," she added.

A chill ran down Rintaro's spine as he looked into her dark, emotionless eyes. He took a step backward. His breath felt constricted, entangled in a myriad of invisible spider threads.

There was no doubt that this adversary was operating on another level. Up until now, he'd sensed the presence of a soul in each of the foes he'd come up against. Or rather, each had had their own way of thinking about books. Finding that had been the clue, the way out of the labyrinth.

But the woman before him now was a steel wall: hard and shiny and impenetrable. There was no clue, no doorway in, just a deep, unfathomable coldness. The usual Rintaro would immediately have raised the white flag, turned on his heels, and fled. As his blood began to run colder in his veins, Rintaro looked down at his feet, hoping to find the tabby cat at his side, but there was no sign of it. He could have found ten or twenty good reasons to run away right then and there.

Instead, he held his ground, putting all the strength he could muster into steadying his trembling knees. This time he hadn't just come along on the spur of the moment; he had a purpose.

"Welcome to Natsuki Books," said the woman, flexing her fingers slightly. "I hope you enjoyed my little stage production. How was your journey?"

"I've come to get Sayo back."

The woman merely narrowed her eyes.

"I've come to get Sayo back," he repeated, but the woman's expression didn't change.

"Really? You're not as clever as I thought you'd be," she said, sighing. "You say the most obvious things. No trace of originality whatsoever."

"'Guy don't need no sense to be a nice fella. Seems to me sometimes it jus' works the other way around. Take a real smart guy and he ain't hardly ever a nice fella,'" said Rintaro.

"Steinbeck? What did you quote him for?"

"I'd say it's a very sharp observation. You seem like a real smart one yourself."

The woman stopped moving her hands and turned her emotionless eyes on Rintaro.

"I take back what I just said. It appears you have a wonderful sense of humor. Inviting you here was apparently worth the effort."

"You know, I have no idea what your intentions are, but I'll try to be polite. Thank you for having me."

"My, you have a shorter temper than rumor would have it. I'd heard you were a nice boy. Not the sort to trade barbs."

Fair point, thought Rintaro. Even though his heart was racing, his mind was unusually clear. It was powered by his anger.

"I'll ask you one more time. Let Sayo go. I don't know what business you have with me, but she has absolutely nothing to do with it."

"My business with you is straightforward. I just wanted to talk to you," said the woman.

Rintaro was flummoxed.

"But if you wanted to talk to me, you could have just asked me to come. Why bother kidnapping Sayo? If you have so much spare time on your hands that you can relax on a fancy sofa all day, or lead a horse and carriage around fountains in a park, why can't you just drop in at Natsuki Books? I'd even treat you to a cup of my grandfather's Assam tea."

"Don't think I haven't thought about it. But if I turned up out of the blue, would you have taken me seriously?"

"Taken you seriously?" Rintaro asked.

"I want to have a serious conversation. I'm not interested in gut reactions or platitudes or lazy attitudes. I want to observe a young man who truly loves books talking seriously about them."

The woman raised both corners of her mouth in a smile. It was a beautiful smile—but as cold as ice.

Rintaro shuddered as if a frozen hand had brushed his neck. Then, as if to repress once again that nagging urge to flee, he began to talk.

"I'll ask you again: Did you take Sayo in order to talk to me?"

"Yes, I did. And looking at you here right now, it looks like I made the right decision."

Rintaro took a deep breath.

Things were moving at her pace. He didn't even know if that was a bad thing or not. What he knew for certain was that it wasn't advisable to let his emotions get the better of him; he needed to think with his head on straight. Especially if the woman wanted to have a serious conversation.

The woman didn't seem satisfied by Rintaro's sudden silence. She raised her right hand and indicated that he should sit on the sofa opposite her.

Rintaro didn't move, so the woman looked at him curiously.

"I see. Well, I believe you'll be more comfortable sitting here."

With a snap of her fingers, the plush sofa melted away and was replaced by a small wooden stool. It was the very same battered old stool that Rintaro always sat on back at the bookshop.

Every aspect of her performance had been carefully devised. But there was not a hint of warmth or consideration for the boy who was trying mightily to stay standing. Every one of her actions was quite simply the shortest means to achieving her goal.

Rintaro realized that to fight it was pointless. He sat down on the stool.

"Okay—what do you want me to talk about?"

"So impatient! But I get it, you're a boy worried about his girlfriend. I forgive you."

She tossed out the words in a matter-of-fact way.

"Would you care to join me for a little movie?" she asked, snapping her fingers again. A large white projector screen appeared in front of the bookcases to Rintaro's right.

"Here's the first one . . ."

As she spoke, an image of a magnificent gate in a long stone wall appeared on the screen. Before Rintaro had time to search his memory for the familiar scene, the camera passed through the gate and on into the mansion beyond. Entering through the traditional Japanese door, it passed through corridors lined with traditional ink paintings, stuffed deer and statues of Venus, and a general mishmash of decorations. Finally, it stopped at the figure of a man sitting on the engawa veranda.

The first time Rintaro had met this man he had been dressed in a brilliant white suit, but now he was wearing a worn shirt and gazed blankly at the garden. The old arrogant overconfidence that had once filled him was gone, and he sat watching the carp swim in the garden pond. By his side were a few books, their covers all creased and wrinkled as if they had been read over and over.

"Look familiar?"

"Yes, it's the first labyrinth."

"Right. And this is the result of saving those books. After all his book collection was released, his reading habits took a turn for the worse. Suddenly, this energetic critic who had read over fifty thousand books was no longer impressive, and his loyal following quickly lost interest in him. The position he had worked to build for himself was taken over by another man who had read sixty thousand books, and now he is a shadow of his former self. He has lost status and honor, and all he does every day is sit and stare at his garden."

The woman looked indifferently at Rintaro. After a moment she gestured to the left-hand bookshelf and a new screen appeared.

"Let's see the next one."

With those words, an image appeared on the screen of a huge space filled with white columns. The space had a high arched ceiling and polished stone floor. The bookshelves that covered all the walls were filled with books and there were narrow passageways and staircases leading off in every direction. It was the second labyrinth.

However, the main library, once filled with men and women in white coats scurrying around with books in their arms, was now deserted. Moreover, there were random books and papers lying around, giving the impression that the place was abandoned. It looked completely deserted, except for one lone figure sitting at a desk in front of one of the massive bookcases.

The camera approached to reveal the chubby middle-aged scholar. When Rintaro and his friends had visited him, he'd been absorbed in his research in his underground office; now he sat forlornly at a table in the corner of the room, looking as if his soul had left his body. His stubble had grown and he stared down at the single small book he held in his hand.

"This genius devised a game-changing speed-reading system in response to our modern times. Now, he's totally abandoned his research to spend hours on end reading one single book. This gifted academic—who used to be able to read ten books in a day—has become an ordinary person. These days, he takes a whole month to finish one. His own books once took the world by storm. But now they've stopped selling, and the requests for lectures that once came pouring in have dried up completely."

"What exactly are you showing me here?" said Rintaro.

"I'm showing you the gap between idealism and reality. And I'm not done yet."

The woman waved her hand upward toward the ceiling. A third screen had appeared, displaying a tall skyscraper. It was the third labyrinth.

The perspective moved through the corridors of the huge, gray building to the familiar scene of the company president's office with its three sides of windows. Or at least it must have been the same room, but it had been given a complete makeover. The chandelier, the red velvet curtains, and the plush sofa set were all gone, giving the room a much simpler appearance. The space was packed instead with men in red, blue, or black suits, noisily conversing.

"This will put the company out of business!" yelled a man in a red suit.

"Books that aren't selling need to be taken out of print immediately."

"Wasn't it you who told us that readers are looking for something provocative and easy to read?"

The men in suits all hurled their complaints in the direction of an elderly gentleman, small in stature. The company president, once so laid-back in his demeanor, now sat with his hands on top of his bowed head.

"The president changed the company's policy. He stopped putting poor sellers out of print, and even started reprinting some older, hard-to-find titles that had been abandoned. As a result, the company's performance went into a decline, and he's under pressure to step down as president."

The woman turned her eyes from the ceiling and back onto Rintaro.

"This is all the result of your glorious adventures," she said in a cold voice. "What do you think?"

"It's terrible," Rintaro managed to squeak out.

The room was chilly. The cold had seeped all the way into Rintaro's body and was oozing down his back. An uncomfortable feeling of nausea seemed to block his whole chest.

"Your words have had a great effect on them, and their circumstances, too. But do you believe it was a good outcome?"

"Well, they didn't look very happy."

"So would you say you've done something reprehensible?"

"What are you trying to tell me?"

"I'm not telling you. I want to hear you say it." Her voice was quiet. "I don't have any definitive answers as to what's right and what's wrong. Maybe in the end that's the reason I called you here. You confronted those three men in order to save books. You dared to exchange words with them and as a result had a lasting impact on their philosophy. You succeeded in changing their values, but as a result, they're all now in trouble. If they have to suffer like that, what was the point of what you did?"

Rintaro had never given that question much thought. It'd be fair to say he'd never expected to be asked.

Rintaro had never had a game plan—he was simply expressing his own opinions. He hadn't really expected the three adversaries to change their ways, especially not to this extent. And he had never imagined that anyone could end up suffering as a result of his words.

Rintaro stared at the three screens in total bewilderment.

"It's a sad old world, don't you think?" said the woman, staring off into space. "People accessorize themselves with books, or stuff themselves with their knowledge and then toss them away. Others think if they pile the books up high enough, they'll be able to see further. But—"

The woman looked at Rintaro. Her eyes were beautiful, but there was nothing behind them. They were like glass beads.

"Is that how it should be?"

Emotionless, she observed Rintaro's confusion. The dark light in her eyes was unreadable. She stood there simply as if she had the right to receive an answer to her question.

"W-Why?" Rintaro finally said, stuttering. "Why are you asking me that?"

"I don't know. Why am I? I thought you might have some fascinating answer for me, that's all."

"Why would I? I'm just some hikikomori. I never really go out into the world."

"But you've been working so hard to save all those books, and you've actually succeeded. These days one rarely sees anyone with such a strong connection to books."

"Strong connection?"

"That's right. People like you and your grandfather are rare. I used to know many like you, but over the past two thousand years everything has changed."

Rintaro thought for a moment he had misheard.

"Two thousand years?"

"Well, about one thousand eight hundred to be exact. That's when I was born. So much time has passed since then."

Rintaro was flabbergasted. The full weight of the cat's phrase "books become imbued with a tremendous power" had been far beyond his imagination. There were not many books that had managed to survive for eighteen hundred years. And even for Rintaro, book lover extraordinaire, there were very few examples of books that still retained a great power after all that time.

The woman ignored Rintaro's amazement and kept on talking.

"In the past it was a matter of course that books had souls. Everybody who read books knew that they did, and they would exchange souls with each other. Back then, there weren't all that many people who could get their hands on books, but those who did supported me with unwavering minds, and I supported them back. I miss that time. It was truly glorious."

"But that—"

"I know it must be hard for you to believe."

The woman's murmur cut Rintaro off.

"I rarely encounter a book with a soul nowadays. What's more, nobody even knows that books used to have souls. The word 'book' has come to mean no more than a bunch of paper with type on it. This is not just about the masses of books that are being read and then thrown away. Even I, who for many centuries have been read by people all over the world, have rarely met anyone who really takes me seriously. Even now, I'm still touted as 'the most widely read book in the world,' but in reality, no one cares about me anymore. I'm locked away, cut into pieces, sold off at a discount. All the things that you have seen on your journeys are happening to me. I've managed to surmount the barriers of two thousand years of time; and of two thousand different languages, and it's even happening to me."

The woman closed her eyes as if trying to suppress her pain.

"I'll be honest with you."

Her thin, almost bloodless lips quivered.

"I'm losing my power. I used to talk about all kinds of important things with all sorts of people, but now I'm starting to forget what I used to talk about. If I forget completely, I'll become just another bundle of paper, just like all those little books containing nothing but information and entertainment."

The woman opened her eyes again.

"It's so very sad. And in my sadness I became curious as to what you were thinking. Why you journeyed through all those labyrinths. You've become quite the celebrity here in this world."

Rintaro couldn't decide whether the last sentence was the woman's attempt at humor, or whether she actually meant what she said. Either way, the weight of the question was the same.

He looked down at his feet. There was no easy reply and yet there were thoughts bubbling up in his mind that he did not want to silence. He reached up and touched his right hand to the frame of his glasses. He shut his eyes.

Once his eyes were closed, the familiar comfort of the round stool transported him back to Natsuki Books. It didn't matter that he was sitting in a fake, reconstructed version of the shop, his mind easily drifted back to where he was most at home.

The seasoned old bookshelves, the retro light fittings, the wooden latticed door that blocked out most of the sunlight, and the silver bell that swung to and fro every time a customer came in. His memory gradually filled the shelves with each of the books he had read.

The Brothers Karamazov, *The Grapes of Wrath*, *The Count of Monte Cristo*, *Gulliver's Travels* . . . Rintaro could recall the exact location of every single book he had read, and as he traced them in his mind, he felt a wave of calm rush through his body.

"I can't—" Rintaro faltered, but he did his best to string his words together.

"I don't know the answer. But I do know that books have helped me many times. I'm the kind of person who tends to dwell on the past, and I give up way too easily, but somehow, I've made it this far because books keep me going."

He stared down at the polished wood floor as he picked the words one by one from the depths of his mind.

"You made some good points, but books are more powerful than you think. Even though so many books are disappearing, there are just as many that survive."

He looked up. The woman was still sitting there, motionless. Rintaro continued, looking at the eyes that never seemed to focus on any particular spot.

"My grandpa always used to say that books have tremendous power. I don't know how things were two thousand years ago, but these days I'm surrounded by fascinating books. I live with them every day. So—"

"Pity."

All of a sudden a cold wind picked up. It was faint, but it had enough strength to cut off Rintaro's speech. His feverish tones were immediately chilled to subzero temperature. The woman's next words struck a final blow.

"You've disappointed me."

Rintaro shivered. He was staring into a dark void. It was a peculiar kind of darkness that lurked behind the woman's eyes. Perhaps it was sorrow, perhaps despair. Whatever it was, it was a bleak emotion, an abyss that swallowed up everything. It was a force that left a mere high school student like Rintaro utterly defenseless.

"Thoughts alone can't change the world."

Her tone was resigned. She had given up.

"I've heard plenty of juvenile idealism, tons of lukewarm optimism. Over and over through the years. I'm tired of it. Because nothing ever changes."

As she spoke, the woman's voice gradually became lower and deeper, and there was a shift in the air. Her eyes stared vacantly, and the lightly crossed legs and hands that rested on them were pale and bloodless. She was like a waxwork figure—fixed to the sofa with nothing moving but her lips. Although she had the form of one, what sat before Rintaro was no longer even a woman. She had turned into a giant crouching being, filled with a dark emotion that had no outlet.

"I've seen all kinds of temporary fixes, stopgap measures. Easy compromises that do nothing but defer the problem. There have been silly debates between smug, self-satisfied people. From time to time the dangers facing books were brought up, but there was nothing we could do to slow the currents. We ended up being swept away. Just like those three people you met who changed their philosophy on life, and ended up losing their place in this world."

She exhaled, and with it the oppressive presence seemed ever so slightly to shrink. Rintaro finally remembered to breathe. Sweat had begun to bead on his forehead.

"When I first heard the rumors about a book-loving boy running around rescuing books, I thought perhaps he would have some words of wisdom for us. Not that I believed it would change anything, but I thought perhaps he could give us a hint of how we might regain that power that we've lost."

She turned her hollow eyes back on Rintaro.

"But it seems I've overestimated you."

Her white hand fluttered slightly.

"You should go back to where you came from."

She waved her hand and something banged behind Rintaro. The wooden door of the shop had opened. Time to embark on his return journey. But Rintaro couldn't even raise his head, let alone get up from his stool. He stayed pinned to the spot.

"We're done here."

The woman's voice was frigid.

She got to her feet and, as if she'd lost interest in Rintaro completely, turned and headed toward the back of the shop. Rintaro raised his head slightly to see the back wall melt away and a passageway open up. This time there were no bookshelves, overhead lamps, nothing—just a dark, endless corridor. The only sound was the dull clacking of the woman's shoes as she slowly faded into the distance.

"I can go home . . ."

Rintaro's mind roamed as if in search of something.

As he watched the woman walk away, he wondered why he was hesitating. His best arguments had been dismissed, his best ideas ridiculed, and his pride literally blown away by a chill wind, but at least nothing had happened to actually hurt him. He was free to slink away, shoulders slumped, and go back to his humdrum existence. He could forget about what happened in those mysterious labyrinths of books. There was only so much a high school kid could do after all. He wasn't a superhero—he was just some moody, gloomy bookworm who happened to make his way to Wonderland. Although this time he could take credit for navigating his way through a series of complicated discussions, he was and always would be a hopeless shut-in, a hikikomori.

With a slightly smug look on his face and an ingrained acceptance of his fate, he had always suppressed what was there in his mind and his heart. That was how he had always lived his life, and he'd been doing just fine, thank you.

And wasn't that good enough?

But then—

"No, that's not good enough," he muttered to himself.

Somewhere in the depths of his mind there was a glimmer of something bright. The main reason he was here—it was as if he had managed to haul a sinking treasure chest back to the surface of the ocean.

Sayo!

His head shot up, and he shuddered in horror. The sound of retreating footsteps was fading quickly. He jumped up.

"Wait! Please."

He yelled it with all his strength, but his voice was swallowed up by the long dark corridor. The sound of the woman's footsteps continued farther into the distance.

"Where's Sayo? Please give her back!"

His voice echoed hopelessly. There was no reply besides the ever-fainter footsteps.

Rintaro turned and looked at the latticed door behind him. It was wide open as if to say, "Look, here's the way out! Go through me and everything will be back to normal. Ordinary, depressing, constricted, but at least there's no need to work up your courage. You don't even need self-respect."

Rintaro imagined himself sitting in a warm, cozy bookshop. And yet his feet didn't budge. The goal of this journey hadn't been to get himself home quickly. He couldn't ignore his real purpose.

He closed his eyes, clenched his fists, and turned his back on the doorway. He began to walk in the direction of the dark corridor at the back of the room.

As he entered, everything turned pitch-black. He couldn't see anything, even his own feet. It was impossible to hurry—he could only depend on the sensation of the hard floor beneath his shoes, and the regular tap-tap sound that they made.

Sweat broke out on his back. He didn't look around, not because he was calm and confident, but because he knew he might freak out if he couldn't see an exit. Deep in his mind negative emotions simmered—fear, regret, self-loathing. If he let them bubble up now, they might boil over and then there would be nothing he could do. Rintaro tried to keep himself calm by thinking of other things. He thought about his school life, his preparations to move, his friendly aunt, the memory of his kind and gentle grandfather and all the books on his shelves, the enigmatic smile on the face of the tabby cat, and the laughter of his classmates.

He stared straight ahead and kept on walking.

He couldn't make out the figure of the woman, but he could still hear the sound of her footsteps. At least they weren't getting any farther away. The anxiety in his heart began to subside.

His stride began to gain some strength. As he walked, he started to talk to nobody in particular.

"You know, I've been thinking about books."

His voice rang out in the darkness.

No reply came. Just the monotonous click-clack of shoes in the distance, regular as the ticking of a clock.

"I've been wondering, exactly what is this power that books possess? Grandpa used to say it all the time: *books have tremendous power*. But what is that power really?"

As he spoke a strange heat began to burn deep inside

him—like a dormant fire that smoldered on despite all attempts to douse it.

"Books can give us knowledge, wisdom, values, a view of the world, and so much more. The joy of learning something you didn't know before, and seeing things in a whole new way is exciting. But somehow I believed they gave us something more important than that."

Rintaro tried to scoop up all the diverse thoughts that came fluttering into his mind like snowflakes, and turn them into words. Each time he thought he'd captured one, it melted away, but he kept on walking deep in thought, determined to express even a part of what he wanted to say.

"I don't believe I have any special powers, and that includes the power to change anything. But if there is one thing I am good at, it's talking about books. And I still have plenty to say. I've been thinking over the topic of the power of books for a long time now, and I believe I've found an answer."

Rintaro came to an abrupt halt staring into the darkness.

"Books teach us how to care about others."

His voice wasn't loud, but it still resonated.

The footsteps stopped.

There was a silence so deep that it seemed to swallow everything. Rintaro peered into the darkness but he couldn't see the woman. Undaunted, he continued to speak to the presence he knew was out there.

"Books are filled with human thoughts and feelings. People suffering, people who are sad or happy, laughing with joy. By reading their words and their stories, by experiencing them together, we learn about the hearts and minds of other people besides ourselves. Thanks to books, it's possible to learn not only about the people around us every day, but people living in totally different worlds."

It was still quiet. The footsteps hadn't resumed. Rintaro took this as an encouraging sign and continued talking.

"Don't hurt anyone. Never bully people weaker than yourself. Help out those in need. Some would say that these rules are obvious. But the truth is, the obvious is no longer obvious in today's world. What's worse is that some people even ask why. They don't understand why they shouldn't hurt other people. It's not a simple thing to explain. It's not logical. But if they read books they will understand. It's far more important than using logic to explain something. Human beings don't live alone, and a book is a way to show them that."

Rintaro did his best to explain to the invisible listener.

"I think the power of books is that—that they teach us to care about others. It's a power that gives people courage and also supports them in turn."

Rintaro broke off for a moment, biting his lip.

"Because you seem to have forgotten," he resumed with all the strength he could muster, "I'm going to say it as loud as I can. Empathy—that's the power of books."

His voice reverberated in the pitch-black space.

As the sound faded away, the air seemed to brighten, and before he knew it his vision was restored. Rintaro found himself back in the same strange replica of Natsuki Books. Beside him was the stool he'd been sitting on, and in front of him the sofa, the woman standing behind it as if she'd been there all along. The entrance door was still wide open, but the pitch-black passageway at the back of the shop was nowhere to be seen. There was nothing but a simple wooden wall. The three screens still showed the three men from the labyrinths and nothing had changed with them.

Was the walk through the passageway a dream? Rintaro could no longer tell for sure how much of this was true.

But one thing had changed. And that was Rintaro himself.

"I'm sorry," he said with a bow of his head. "You told me to leave, but I can't go yet. You haven't given Sayo back."

The woman didn't answer. There was still no hint of any light or warmth in her eyes, just a chill enough to make anyone shudder.

And yet, Rintaro didn't panic. His opponent was much greater than he was. And there was no way for him to express all his thoughts right away. But the fact that she had stopped and turned around to listen to him was significant.

"So many people are trying to destroy our precious books," she said. "If books are destroyed, they lose their power. No matter how powerful they are, books are regularly locked away, cut up, sold off, and eventually die. And I'm sure in the future this will only continue."

"Yes, but they won't die out."

At Rintaro's gentle words, the woman's hair seemed to quiver slightly.

"Even if you try to destroy a book, it doesn't disappear that easily. Right now, in places all over the world, people have connections to books. The fact that you are here with me now is the best proof of that."

The woman's eyebrows moved ever so slightly in surprise. That was the first expression that had ever crossed her face.

There was a pause.

Then as if it had been waiting for a moment like this, a voice came out of nowhere.

"Well said, boy."

It was a male voice, strong and confident.

Rintaro looked around the room, but there was no one there but the woman.

"I knew you had it in you! I'm impressed."

Rintaro realized the voice was coming from his right and was startled to see the man on the screen smiling at him— the one from the first labyrinth. He was still sitting on his porch, sipping tea.

"You've nothing to lose, young man. Just be brave and shout it at her. Hey, you! You talk a big game, but you're just sitting there looking down at the world and doing nothing about it. You're the one resting on your laurels."

The man looked amused at Rintaro's shocked expression.

"Young man, it's very difficult to get things to change. But you weren't afraid to attack me with your best words. I owe you my thanks. Ever since, I've been discovering something new and surprising every day. As you said, I didn't truly love books back then. Was surrounded by so many books that I'd failed to notice that within each one was a boundless world.

That said, my biggest discovery has nothing to do with books at all."

He took another leisurely sip from his teacup.

"I've discovered that my wife truly makes a wonderful cup of tea."

He chuckled pleasantly in a way that made Rintaro feel warm inside. As he continued laughing, another voice came from Rintaro's left.

"Have confidence, my young guest."

Rintaro turned his attention to the left-hand screen, where the scholar from the second labyrinth sat watching him. Chubby-cheeked, he smiled at Rintaro, whose mouth had fallen open. His eyes sparkled.

"Weren't you the one who fast-forwarded my Beethoven cassette tape? Remember the courage you showed then!"

He gave a gentle nod and smiled again.

"Walk with courage the path you have chosen. Don't be one of those bystanders who complains that nothing ever changes. Continue your journey, just as Melos kept running to the end."

The woman's thin eyebrows furrowed slightly.

"Thoughts alone can't change the world," she repeated.

"But don't you think we should give it a try?"

The voice came from the ceiling above Rintaro. He looked up to see the company president had gotten up from his chair and was addressing the crowd of men in suits.

"It's not a question of logic. It's about being proud of who we are."

The president raised a surprisingly large hand to quell the voices of protest.

"Didn't you all join this company because you loved books?" he asked them. His voice wasn't loud, but it was energetic. The men immediately stopped their clamoring.

"Then put aside all this logic and rationale. Let's talk about our ideals instead. First of all, it's our privilege to publish books."

The men in suits seemed to stand a little straighter.

Rintaro shifted his gaze from up at the ceiling and toward the woman.

"It doesn't matter how slight or superficial it is, a change is a change."

This time, the woman met Rintaro's gaze without looking away. He looked her straight in the eye as he added:

"Why is it that although we all believe in the power of books, you don't seem to?"

The woman didn't move. Rintaro's words faded away and the two of them were once more enveloped in silence.

This time the silence was not easy to break. It was deep and heavy and filled the space around their feet like a silent blanket of snow. Eventually it became so oppressive that it was hard to breathe. This was the heaviest silence that Rintaro had experienced in this final labyrinth.

Finally, the woman closed her eyes.

"I hate this . . ." she murmured. "From time to time I come across people who talk this way. It means I can't completely give up hope."

As always, her voice was toneless and impossible to read. Yet there was a very slight inflection that hadn't been there before. Rintaro was startled to see a soft light flicker a moment in her eyes. It was brief, and immediately faded back into the darkness of her pupils, but he was sure it had been there.

"Empathy . . ." said the woman to herself. "That's not a bad idea."

She turned, as if she had noticed something behind her. A light had begun to fill the bookshop, starting from the far wall and spreading farther and farther, illuminating the dim interior. The bookshelves and the screens began to take on a faint glow.

"Time's up," said the woman.

"What time?"

"I've done some pretty reckless things—I can't go on like this forever."

She continued to stare at the bright light that was filling the bookshop.

"You really should leave this time. If you don't go now, you may never be able to get home. It's okay. You don't need to worry about your girlfriend."

As he nodded his understanding, the room got steadily lighter around him.

"So this is goodbye?"

"Yes . . . It's been . . ."

The woman seemed to hesitate a moment.

"It's been a pleasure."

"It was nice to meet you, too," said Rintaro.

He bowed deeply, and the woman acknowledged it with a nod.

"You really do have some admirable qualities," she said. "But were you humoring me just then?"

"No. Not at all. Thanks to meeting you, I've realized something very important."

The woman watched Rintaro as he bowed deeply once again, clearly expressing his gratitude.

"What pleasant parting words."

With that the woman raised her hand and the three screens all vanished, revealing once again the sad, empty bookshelves. But then she reached out and touched the bookcases. This time in a rush of bluish-white light, books began to appear one after the other on the shelves, until the shelves were packed full of books, all arranged in proper order.

"I think these suit the space much better," said the woman without smiling.

Rintaro realized that this was her way of saying thank you.

"Me, too," he said. "I think this is much better."

He smiled at the woman, and, expressionless, she nodded back. It was almost imperceptible, but it was a nod.

The light grew stronger, enveloping the bookcases, the sofa, and the two of them. Rintaro could do nothing but stand there.

The woman's thin, bloodless lips moved as if she were saying something, but the words failed to reach Rintaro's ears. Then she turned her back on him. Rintaro was unexpectedly impressed by the ease of her demeanor, as she walked away with no sign of regret.

"Thank you."

As Rintaro let the pure white light wash over him, he was sure that these had been her own parting words.

How much time had passed? It was hard to say.

Rintaro found himself sitting on the familiar wooden floor of Natsuki Books. In his arms, sleeping peacefully, was his classmate. At the back end of the shop was the simple wooden wall, and outside the front door, the street was bright with a dusting of snow.

"Sayo?" he whispered, and her eyes immediately popped open.

"Natsuki . . . ?"

Rintaro sighed with relief at the sound of her voice. Looking up at him, Sayo waited a moment before speaking.

"You okay?"

"I think that's my line."

Rintaro smiled wryly, and Sayo smiled back at him. It was that familiar charming smile that she gave him whenever she dropped by to see him. She glanced around the shop.

"Looks like you got to bring me home, then."

"That was the agreement."

Rintaro took Sayo's hand and stood up. He was facing her

with his back to the door. The soft light shining in through the latticework from the snowy exterior made her look more radiant than ever.

"Is *Welcome back* the right thing to say in this situation?" Rintaro asked.

Sayo shook her head.

"Nope."

She smiled at Rintaro's confused expression.

"You should say *Merry Christmas*."

This was an expression a little unfamiliar to Rintaro, but it had a lovely ring to it.

"Merry Christmas," he repeated with a smile.

HOW
IT ALL
ENDED

lematis was his grandpa's favorite flower. The old man had a particular love of the deepest, richest blue variety. Rintaro recalled his grandfather's face squinting in the bright sun of early summer as he admired the open petals. Its Japanese name, literally "iron lined flower," seemed to suit its elegant straight lines and gentle curves better than its botanical name. He remembered how his grandfather had been unusually talkative as he filled the plant pots in front of the shop with clematis.

I can do this, he thought, as he began to water the plants. He felt more at peace than he had lately.

It had been three months since his grandfather had passed away. The seasons had moved on, bringing with them a change in scenery. The snow under the eaves had melted, the plum blossoms had flowered, and now the buds on the cherry trees were about to burst open.

As the seasons flowed by along their regular course, Rintaro had been keeping his own regular schedule. Every morning at 6:00 a.m. he'd open up the wooden latticed door to air out the little shop. He'd take a broom and sweep the front steps, water the plants, now covered in fresh new leaves, and then sweep out the interior of the shop.

"You're really on top of it."

Just as he was about done with the cleaning, he heard Sayo's cheerful voice, and she walked in carrying her black instrument case. Rintaro had recently learned that she played the bass clarinet. He'd never heard of the instrument but reliable sources told him that Sayo was the only one in the band who could play it.

"You do this day in, day out."

She sat down on a stool in the middle of the shop.

"Is it really necessary to clean the shop every day?"

Rintaro laughed as he took the books off the shelf and dusted them one by one.

"It's fine. You and I are different people. I don't have any club activities to go to in the mornings. New books catch my interest every time I clean, so it's a lot of fun."

"You're such a nerd."

Sayo was being as blunt as ever, which Rintaro always found refreshing.

"But this book really is terrible, don't you think?"

As she spoke, Sayo produced a thick hardback book from her shoulder bag.

"I just don't get it at all."

Rintaro grimaced. It was Gabriel García Márquez's *One Hundred Years of Solitude*. He'd started off recommending Jane Austen, moved on to Stendhal, Gide, Flaubert—all love stories, thinking they'd be enjoyable reads for her—but just last week Sayo had announced she was ready to try other genres. Rintaro had suggested García Márquez.

"Did you really read this whole thing?" she asked him.

"Of course. It was a while back, though."

"Yeah, you're weird. I can't understand a word of it. It's too difficult."

"That's good."

Rintaro chuckled as he knocked the dust off the nearest bookshelf. Sayo stared at him with a puzzled look on her face.

"Why's it good?"

"If you find it difficult, it's because it contains something that is new to you. Every difficult book offers us a brand-new challenge."

"What are you talking about?"

Sayo didn't look convinced.

"If you find a book easy to read, that means it's all stuff that you already know," he went on. "That's why it's easy. If you find it difficult, then that's proof it's something brand new."

As Rintaro laughed, Sayo observed him as if he were some kind of exotic animal.

"You really are a weirdo, aren't you?"

"That's a bit mean."

"But it's not a bad thing."

Sayo rested her forehead in her hand and stared at Rintaro.

"Actually, it's pretty cool," she said.

Rintaro's hand suddenly stopped moving. He glanced in Sayo's direction and saw her grinning at him.

"Your ears have gone all red," she said.

"I'm an innocent. Unlike some."

"What do you mean, 'innocent'? You're always reading novels like *Lolita* and *Madame Bovary*. I think you're really a secret pervert."

"If you're gonna be like that I'm not selling you any more books."

"I'm just kidding," said Sayo cheerfully, getting to her feet. However, she didn't make for the front door, wandering instead over to the back of the shop.

"It really does just stop here, doesn't it?"

"If it didn't, we'd really have a problem."

"It would be a problem, but it's still kind of a pity. It just feels like it was all a dream now."

Sometimes Rintaro thought it must have been a dream. But even if it had been, there was one thing that was perfectly clear to him now. He was not alone.

"I've decided I'd like to stay at the bookshop."

It was Christmas Eve, one hour before the moving van was about to arrive when Rintaro had finally said those words.

He'd thought it was a really outrageous thing to say, but his aunt hadn't been particularly surprised. She'd simply folded her arms and returned her nephew's gaze. The awkward silence that followed felt long, but it quite possibly lasted only a few moments.

"Something happened, didn't it, Rin-chan?" she said quite calmly.

The question came as a surprise to Rintaro. The aunt smiled at the boy's confusion.

"Don't worry about it. I don't suppose you're about to explain the whole thing to a middle-aged aunt you barely know."

Of course, Rintaro couldn't tell her about his bizarre adventures with a talking cat. More than that he hadn't really come to terms at that point with how the experience had changed him. But whatever it was, he had decided it was time to strike out on his own. There was no such thing as having no choice. Rintaro knew that now. There were many roads to choose from. What was important was not to let yourself roll along aimlessly, but to pick a road.

How can I move on if I don't believe in myself? Deep in that labyrinth, Rintaro had asked himself that question. His words turned into strength and he felt able to keep going alone.

His aunt saw that he was not about to speak, so she had continued.

"Living on your own isn't going to be too much for you?"

"Too much?"

"I mean, is it because you hate the thought of living with a distant relative? You're not just making this up on the spot to get out of it?"

"No, that's not it."

"Are you sure?"

"Definitely," he replied, briefly and with complete confidence.

His aunt stayed there for a while, her arms still crossed. Finally, she gave a decisive nod.

"Okay then. If you accept my three conditions, then I might agree."

"What conditions?"

"Number one is that you attend school."

Uh-oh, Rintaro thought. So she knew that he hadn't been going . . .

"The second condition is that you call me three times a week. Just to let me know you're okay. And then the third condition . . ."

She unfolded her arms, put her hands on her generous hips, and leaned in toward him.

"If you have any trouble, don't try to solve everything by yourself, ask me for help. It's not easy for a high school student to live by himself."

Rintaro was caught off guard. His aunt was kind; everything she did was out of consideration for her nephew. If she had been in the bookshop back then, he just knew she would have been able to see the cat and the mysterious passageway.

"Calling you three times a week might be a bit tricky."

"Hmm, I wonder which is trickier—that or calling a moving company to cancel a contract one hour before they're due to arrive? Would you care to swap places?"

His aunt was clever, too.

"Thank you," said Rintaro, bowing his head. He heard his aunt murmur to herself: "Look at you, Rintaro. You've turned out just like your grandfather."

There was no better compliment.

——

"Every difficult book offers us a brand-new challenge, huh?" said Sayo, staring at her copy of *One Hundred Years of Solitude*.

"By the way, García Márquez happens to be one of Akiba's favorite authors," said Rintaro. "I bet he's read all these titles."

"Whatever—don't tell me that. Now I feel even less like reading them."

She glared at Rintaro as she put the heavy book back in her bag.

"But if it doesn't pick up, I'm going to hold you responsible."

"Gabriel García Márquez wrote it, not me."

"But you're the one who recommended it, not Gabriel García Márquez."

His aunt, Sayo—Rintaro marveled at the fact that he was surrounded by such intelligent women.

"Oh no!"

Sayo leapt to her feet. She'd just realized that band practice was about to start. She grabbed her bass clarinet from the table and hurried to the door.

"Natsuki, make sure you come to school today."

"I'm going. I promised my aunt I would."

He walked her to the door and saw that the sky was beautiful and clear. A yellow delivery bicycle went past, bright against the blue of the sky.

Sayo bounded down the steps in front of the shop, but then turned as if she'd forgotten something.

"Hey, do you want to go out for dinner sometime?" she said offhandedly.

Rintaro was completely flustered. He blinked twice as if unable to believe his ears.

"You want to have dinner with me?"

"Yeah."

"Why?"

"Because if I waited for you to ask me it would never happen."

Rintaro got even more flustered. Sayo sighed and shrugged.

"It's all well and good to chat inside the bookshop, but occasionally you need to get a bit of sun or you'll be ill. Do you really want your grandfather in heaven to get worried sick over you?"

"If I go out to dinner with a girl, Grandpa's really going to worry."

(That's what he would have liked to say, had his mind not gone completely blank.)

"If you're okay with it," Rintaro said. It was all he could get out.

"I'll make do," Sayo said. It was a crisp response; there was nothing more to say.

She flashed him the most beautiful smile he'd ever seen and set off down the road. As he listened to her footsteps, Rintaro's mouth fell open.

"Sayo!" he managed to shout.

His classmate turned around.

"Thank you."

His shy voice came out louder than he'd expected.

Sayo seemed surprised. He wasn't normally so direct, but his words were powered by a great depth of feeling.

In fact, he had many feelings for this friend who had dropped in to care for him so many times. He had been struggling with how to express all these to her, but "thank you" seemed to suffice.

Sayo was still standing there, and he raised his voice once again.

"I'm really grateful. So much has been thanks to you."

"What's up with you all of a sudden? Yuck."

"Hey, Yuzuki, looks like you're blushing now."

"I'm not!"

She turned and ran down the road. The bright sunshine fell on Rintaro's back and he felt his uniform warm against his skin. As he stood there seeing Sayo off, he suddenly heard a deep voice in his ear.

"Good luck, Mr. Proprietor."

Startled, Rintaro turned and looked around, but of course there was nobody to be seen. He thought he might have caught a glimpse of the back of a tabby cat disappearing over the fence across the street but he couldn't be certain. The street seemed just the same as it always was.

He stood there for a moment before giving a little smile.

"I'll do my best," Rintaro said. He looked up at the sky.

He would go back inside, finish the cleaning, drink a cup of his usual Assam tea, and read a few pages of a book. When it was time, he would shut up the shop, pick up his schoolbag, and head out to school. Going to school might be dull, but he didn't want to rack up any more absences and make the class rep angry.

Problems remained, and he had yet to completely resolve any of them, but now all he had to do was follow the path he had chosen for himself.

Leaving the latticed door open, he went back into the shop and got out his tea set. He boiled the water in the kettle and poured it into his grandfather's well-used teapot. He heard laughter from out in the street. It was the local primary school kids passing by on their way to school. The presence of more people signaled the beginning of a new day.

Surrounded by the pleasant aroma of tea, Rintaro carefully opened his book.

A gentle breeze brushed the doorbell, and it gave a cheerful ring.

I had always wanted to translate something in the fantasy genre, and this charming tale about books and reading was instantly fascinating to me. Who doesn't love a talking cat?

The Cat Who Saved Books contains four labyrinths, both a classical reference to the ancient Greek myth of Theseus and the minotaur, and a more modern interpretation of the labyrinth as journey of self-discovery. Throughout the novel, Rintaro Natsuki confronts monsters in the form of people who mistreat books, as well as his own demons. Western literature is frequently referenced, but at the same time this book is very Japanese.

Rintaro is a *hikikomori*, a Japanese term that isn't easy to translate into English. Literally meaning to pull inward and confine, the term refers to people, often young men, who have consciously decided to shut themselves away from society, rarely venturing outside to school or work. In 2019 the Japanese government estimated their number at over one million. It can only be assumed that this number has increased over the past couple of years with the onset of COVID-19.

The term *hikikomori* has become more widely recognized in the English-speaking world, making its way into the *Oxford English Dictionary* in 2010. And so I made the decision, rather than translating it, to retain it in the text along with some details to remind the reader of its meaning.

I also retained some other difficult-to-translate Japanese terms, such as traditional Japanese architectural features. There is, for example, the *engawa*, a kind of low wooden veranda that runs around the edge of a traditional Japanese house, and the *fusuma*, a sliding door made from wood and paper.

Impossible to retain, however, is the absence of pronouns in the Japanese language. English requires them for writing and speech to sound natural. Japanese words for "he" or "she" exist but they are rarely used, and never in this novel. We know because it is stated in the text that Rintaro is a boy and Sayo a girl. The cat poses more of a challenge. Never referred to once as "he," "she," or "it," but simply "the cat" or "the tabby," this character's gender is indeterminate.

In truth, the clues are there in its language. There tend to be different masculine and feminine styles of speech in Japanese, and in the original language the cat sounds more like a man than a woman. I could have made the decision to use the male pronoun, and turn the tabby cat into a male talking cat, but I admit to exercising a touch of translator's prerogative. I felt that there was no necessity to add another male character, and that as the original author had not specified a gender, it was reasonable to use a neutral pronoun. Readers will have to make up their own minds.

—Louise Heal Kawai

Reading the novel in Japanese reminded me of certain literary classics from my native country. The author's name, Sosuke Natsukawa, and the protagonist's name, Rintaro Natsuki, are both very old-fashioned names. They recall Natsume Soseki, who's best-known book in Japan is *I Am a Cat* (1906). If this is all a coincidence, it's a very good one.

My work plays with the Western perception of Japanese art. I sometimes heighten the Japanese influence by carefully mimicking the look of traditional *ukiyo-e* painting when I illustrate traditional or historical Japanese stories—a style that originated in seventeenth-century Japan, as a way to capture the hedonistic and sensual delights of the urban entertainment districts. Although the writing style of *The Cat Who Saved Books* was inspired by the old masters of the Japanese literary canon, the book's premise feels very modern. Thus, I went for a slight *ukiyo-e* influence (e.g., the clouds pay homage to iconic painter and printmaker Hokusai's style, whose print *Great Wave Off Kanagawa* you will likely recognize), but the cover is more representative of my own "East meets West" personal style.

The colors intentionally draw on a traditionally Japanese color palette—for example, I chose a reddish-orange rather than a deep red—and I was also inspired by the aged paper seen in old Japanese scrolls. But the books featured are Western books. Most of the books referenced in this novel are Western stories, so I thought that was fitting.

The image was created with ink with a traditional Japanese brush for copying sutras on watercolor paper, then scanned into and digitally colored in Adobe Photoshop.

—Yuko Shimizu

Here ends Sosuke Natsukawa's
The Cat Who Saved Books.

The first edition of this book was printed
and bound at LSC Communications in
Harrisonburg, Virginia, in December 2021.

A NOTE ON THE TYPE

This novel was set in Century Schoolbook, a transitional serif typeface from the Century typeface family. It was designed in 1919 by Morris Fuller Benton for the American Type Founders at the request of Ginn & Company, a textbook publisher. It became widely popular for its readability and has been used to teach North American children how to read for generations.

HARPERVIA

An imprint dedicated to publishing international voices,
offering readers a chance to encounter other lives and other
points of view via the language of the imagination.